MAÑANA IS YESTERDAY

By

IRVING G. TRAGEN

THIS BOOK IS DEDICATED TO
MY LATE WIFE ELE
FROM WHOSE NOTES ON OUR
TOURS IN CENTRAL AMERICA
I FOUND THE TITLE AND INSPIRATION
FOR THIS WORK OF FICTION.

ALL THE CHARACTERS AND INCIDENTS DEPICTED
ARE ELEMENTS OF MY REFLECTIONS
ABOUT THE
DIFFICULT TRANSITION OF CENTRAL AMERICA
FROM ITS COLONIAL AND FEUDALIST PAST
AND
ANY RESEMBLANCE TO A PERSON LIVING OR DEAD
IS
COINCIDENTIAL

A WORD OF APPRECIATION

WRITING A FIRST NOVEL AT 100 YEARS OF AGE HAS BEEN AN AWESOME ADVENTURE. GETTING IT PUBLISHED, HAS BEEN AN IMPOSSIBLE DREAM – UNTIL INCREDIBLY SPECIAL PEOPLE CAME TO MY AID.

THOSE INCREDIBLY SPECIAL PEOPLE ARE ELIANA ALEXANDER AND JOHN NIKITIN, WHO READ MY TEXT, LIKED AND GUIDED ME IN EDITING IT AND GETTING IT PUBLISHED.

ELIANA EVEN USED HER ARTISTRY AND IMAGINATION TO TRANSFORM A VAGUE PERCEPTION IN MY MIND INTO THE COVER OF THIS BOOK.

LET ME ALSO RECOGNIZE THE CONTRIBUTION OF THE LATE DR. HOWARD RUBENSTEIN TO THIS PUBLICATION. HIS ADROIT EYE PRODUCED THE PHOTOGRAPH OF ME ON THE BACK COVER.

THERE ARE NOT ENOUGH WORDS IN THE ENGLISH LANGUAGE TO EXPRESS MY APPRECIATION TO THEM.

CHAPTER 1

The Mercedes Benz eased by the opened iron gate, moved slowly up the circular driveway to the front door of the elegant two-story French Provincial mansion. The bodyguard jumped out of the car on the ready and with gun drawn as Leona waited for the long-time family chauffeur to open the door for her on her arrival home from the tumultuous private meeting of the country's most powerful families.

As she stepped out of the car, all afternoon she sat restlessly, but silently, as the meeting dragged on. Her silence meant that she had acquiesced in taking strong coordinated measures to subvert the electoral process to take place next Sunday and to confront rising social unrest, including demands for higher wages and better living condition by the workers on the coffee fincas though out the country.

She resolutely lifted herself from her usual right corner back seat, took her chauffeur's hand and eased herself from the car to the walkway up to the front door at which her lifelong friend Margarita awaited her. Looking at Leona's face, she reacted, "I presume that It didn't go well."

Leona shrugged her shoulders and half sighed. "Well, I didn't say much. Just listened most of the time. Something inside of me kept me quiet when my mind kept telling me to express my deep concern about using the military in the election Sunday or to deal with the social unrest."

Margarita took her arm as they walked up the staircase to Leona's suite at the end of the hall on the second story. Leona kept saying almost to herself, "I know that the military will keep the status quo and help us get the crops to market, but the real problems remained unresolved, and the bitterness will make it more difficult with the finca people in the future."

Margarita just looked at Leona with sad eyes—she not only sensed the political consequences of subverting the election but she knew the people who were to be silenced at Leona's fincas and ached for them. But, in her role as friend, she had to let Leona offer her a chance to talk. After all, Margarita had a special relationship since Leona had been little more than a baby. They had grown up together and been playmates, but with a great difference between them: Leona was the daughter of the patron, and she was the illegitimate daughter of the cook, more than five years older Leona. Though Margarita was now a lawyer and business associate, she always sensed that wall between them.

As they entered Leona's room, Margarita asked, "What would you like for supper?"

Leona had not thought about food,

only the flow of the meeting. "Not much just some consume and crackers in my room."

Leona turned and half-smiled. Margarita nodded and left. Leona walked deliberately through her office-sitting room into her adjoining large lavender colored bedroom. She stepped out of the Oleg Casino black dress that he had designed personally for her and put on the French silk dressing gown that her maid had laid out on her queen-sized bed. She kept chiding herself for her silence at the meeting as well as the results. She kept hearing the arguments of her primo hermano (first cousin) Luis about our responsibility to lead the people out of the current political unrest and asked herself why she, among the most influential and powerful people in the room, just let it continue. Why, oh why, had she said so little all afternoon when her mind told her there was a better option than military intervention and force. Her concern rose even deeper as she realized that her silence may have created the impression that she condoned the result.

Even though it still was early evening she began her usual nightly ritual of retiring. She placed her jewels in her bedside safe and moved to her dressing table and settled herself in her comfortable chair. She picked up a cloth to wipe off her make-up as she had done now in so many cycles of her life. As she casually droned away at the task in her elegantly appointed high ceiling bedroom, her mind kept focusing on the afternoon and she felt no inner peace.

Then the cloth cleaning her face slipped through her fingers and fell on her lap. As she reached down to retrieve it, she was startled by an image in the mirror-- not her actual nearly 40-year-old self. She instantly recognized that it was she as a freshman at Yale — and that face whispered to her, "Today you betrayed everything you hoped to accomplish in your lifetime."

Chapter 2

Leona was so startled by the image in the mirror that she felt every nerve in her body react. She, Leona Cristina Borakas Suarez Moncada, the usually composed person in charge was shaken to the core.

It was her primo hermano (first cousin) Luis, who pressured her into attending a closed meeting of the Salvadoran Great Families on the eve of Sunday's presidential election. How he played on her sense of duty as the leader of the Suarez Moncada family who played a specially important role in developing the nation and her importance as the head of the family business!

Her reluctance in going to the meeting multiplied when she entered the meeting room and saw that Luis and his die-hard cohorts were running it. She heard Luis pledge to support the electoral process but stressed that the campaign rhetoric had turned "radical" and that it had spawned agitation and unrest on the country's fincas and plantations which were in great part owned by the Great Families present. Then came Luis's agenda: "The radicals must be the stopped and the agitation brought under control so that our country will not be denied the income from the fincas and plantations and the people who depend on us for their livelihood are not denied their sustenance."

After some comments by various members present in support of Luis, one of his cronies warned, "The polls show that the Christian Democratic candidate has an advantage over the Army colonel—and a win would threaten our long-term interests. And I propose that we do everything we can in the next two days to support the colonel and prevent the radical from taking over."

When participants raise questions about the needs for the families to react,

Luis or his cronies would point to their historic role, the political imperative of maintaining the status quo and of ensuring the flow of coffee income for sustaining the nation and meeting the needs of the people-with great emphasis on their duty to serve the people unprepared to care for themselves.

When someone raised a question about how the Americans would react Luis himself replied, "All the American advisers here know me and my friends. They know we are anti soviet and in the cold war now that is all Washington is interested in."

Leona just seemed to absorb the flow of the discussion-almost in limbo. She felt uncomfortable with Luis's arguments which she found contrived and self- serving. But some inner voice kept telling her that she had a duty to the country and the people-and maybe there was a rational base for what Luis was advocating. And, from her recent contacts in Washington Luis was right about an US intervention.

Like clockwork, another crony proposed, "Let us advise our contacts in the military that we consider them part of us, and we will stand behind them in making sure that the radicals don't upset the life of our country."

Leona was well acquainted with chain of command in the military and the support that the Great Families have given them since the country's independence—from one military strongman to the next. She was equally aware of her father and like-minded members of the Great Families had supported the Central American Common Market in the 1950's and 60's to change the feudal economic system and support the broadening of popular participation in the political process. She appreciated the havoc that the military had wreaked in the bloody Soccer War with Honduras only three years earlier that disrupted the Common Market and the political opening. She knew how much the Common Market had enriched so man of the Great families. And she noted how many heads of those Great Families were not present at Luis' meeting. She knew there were progressive officers and the hard-liners in the Army—and knew Luis's ties were to the hard-liners—the ones rumored to have ties to the death squads, committed to politics by assassination. She saw red flags, but still she said nothing.

Yet she failed to react. As the meeting droned on, one part of her brain said that the positions being advocated by Luis and his cronies were wrong and that the Great Families should not contact the military and above all, not interfere with the electoral process—better to get prepared to adapt to change. But another powerful inner voice kept telling her that it was in her best interest to let Luis and his cronies contact the military with the message that the Great Families supported its candidate and the status quo. This ambivalence was so unlike her usual self— the decisive CEO of one of the most successful multinational food enterprises in the region, the graduate of Yale and Harvard Business School and protégé of her father, a member of the powerful Greek international banking family.

Her instinct kept telling her to speak up and scuttle Luis's proposals, her university-trained mind kept telling her that Luis's words are not what they seemed. Were they not subterfuge to protect the interests of the least enlightened feudal landlords? Isn't calling on armed forces to restore public order no more than window-dressing for propping up the traditional power of the least progressive elements of the Great Families?

But another voice kept telling her that Luis's words were a call to responsible action by those who founded the country and brought order and Christ to the poor indigenous people. Didn't they express the essential responsibility of those like "us" with power and means to truly protect "them" from making wrong decisions? Something inside of herself kept saying "we" know what is best for "them."

In her confusion, she endured the afternoon, just listening, never saying a word.

With only scattered resistance to Luis and his cronies, probably in no small part due to her silence, Luis became bolder in his pronouncements and then jolted Leona by proclaiming, "The Great Families have reached a consensus and it is my duty to advise the military that we support their candidate and are prepared to support them in whatever actions they deem necessary to assure that victory. The meeting is adjourned."

Then Leona seemed to wake up. Her ambivalence turned to concern. Luis had taken for himself an authority never endowed by the meeting. He announced that he and his cronies would advise immediately the military of the decision reached and adjourned the meeting forthwith.

Now, she realized what her silence had wrought. She hurried out of the meeting place without speaking to anyone—even to her closest business associates and friends.

As she rode home, she realized that Luis had used her. Anger toward Luis was mixed with a shame had welled up within her. And then the image in the mirror had compounded her unease and so deeply immersed her in thought that she had not heard Margarita knocking at her bedroom door. Deeply concerned, Margarita finally opened the door and asked, "Leona, are you all right?"

Leona was shaking when she realized that Margarita had entered. Coming back to reality, she tried to compose herself as she said, "Oh, yes Margarita, come in."

Margarita was accompanied by the maid pushing the teacart holding Leona's dinner. As she quickly moved into the room, she immediately sensed the turmoil within Leona. She could not recall a time when she had seen Leona so shaken. She looked quizzically at Leona, asking with her eyes if she was indeed all right and if Leona needed someone to talk to.

Leona half-smiled at her and motioned the maid to bring the tea cart over to the dressing table. The cook had prepared the consume, several water cress open-faced sandwiches, a pot of tea and a platter of sliced mangos, papaya and oranges. Leona smiled her thanks.

Margarita looked again into Leona's face and was not satisfied that she was herself. She probably knew her better than anyone else in the universe. Growing up together, she had always looked at Leona more as a sister than the daughter of her employer—and she protected her as if she were. She was Leona's refuge, especially when the child Leona was scolded by her Granmama for any one of a thousand missteps, but most of all for having been her father's daughter, inheriting his coarse Greek features that besmirched the shapely Castilian eyes and nose of the Suarez Moncada blood.

Margarita asked aloud, "Leona are you sure you are all right?"

Leona toying with her food, "I am not sure. The meeting that Luis ran today has unsettled me. For reasons I don't understand, I sat by and let him and his cronies push through an agenda that my mind tells me is not right. I need time to review what happened this afternoon and what to do about it. Right now, all I want is a hot bath. Just leave the cart. I'll nibble at the food as I feel hungry."

Margarita nodded. She and the maid left Leona to herself. Alone again Leona took a few spoonsful of soup and ate a couple of the sandwiches and slices of fruit on the tray-- more to please Margarita and the cook than because she felt hungry. All the time the image in the mirror was burning itself into her memory and forcing her to remember moments in her life which she has stored away since she had grown up. She began remembering images of her childhood and the words of her Grandma that sounded so like the arguments Luis had repeated over and over during the meeting.

Then, she took her leisurely bath, put on a new pair of silk pajamas, and slipped into bed. She was trying to relax, but every corner into which she looked, she saw the image in the mirror. She was about to turn off the lamp on her bed side table when Margarita and the maid came back to remove the teacart. Looking at the concern in Leona's eyes, Margarita asked once again, "Do you need anything? Would talking to me about it help?" – even though she sensed that Leona alone had to come to grips with the malaise that absorbed her.

Leona half-smiled at Margarita as she said, "I have a problem that only I can deal with. I suspect that I won't be sleeping much tonight."

Margarita, on cue said, "Good night. If you need me, just call. Please try to get some rest."

Chapter 3

As soon as Leona stretched out in bed, her mind was drawn back to the details of the afternoon and the source of her ambivalence and disquiet. Where to start unlocking the dilemma that engulfed her? She found herself reliving her life, whisked off to the days of her childhood.

She saw herself back in the Suarez Moncada grand mansion near the center of San Salvador, only a few manzanas (blocks) north of the Central Market, on land granted to her ancestors by the King of Spain. It was one of the most elegant modern constructions in the city, built on the foundations of the once sprawling family home started by the first generation of Suarez Moncada's after their arrival in Cuscatlán at the end of the eighteenth century and then enlarged by their progeny.

The new house, built after 1900, was shielded from the street by a thick, whitewashed adobe wall built on the property line to keep out the unwelcome. It was a two-story Parisian style building with patios and gracious flowered walkways. Behind the front gate was a curved driveway to the front door. Behind the back gate were the stables and servant quarters. The house was equipped with the latest French electrical conveniences and seven bathrooms, bidets and porcelain bath tubs, for each of the family and guest bedrooms. In the center of the house was a formal patio which offered year-round breezes to bedrooms on the second floor and for the salons, dining room, library and master suite on the first.

The home of Leona's childhood was governed by her grandmother—who insisted on being called Granmama. No one ever called by her given name. She was a ramrod who imposed her will on all whom she encountered, including her husband, Leona's grandfather, her surviving children, the family, the numerous servants and Leona.

It was Granmama who set the routine of her young life and impressed upon her the importance of being part of not only her grandfather's Suarez Moncada clan but also that of her own bloodline. Granmama would stand over Leona and in a very stern voice remind her: "You are a young lady whose blood from both sides of your mother's family is noble, from Spanish families to whom the King gave land in Central America hundreds of years ago. Your ancestors civilized this heathen land and brought the Church and order to their lives. It is through my family's blood flowing in your veins that you are a descendant of the great Conquistadores of the 16th century, a true hidalgo ennobled by the King of Spain and grantee of prime lands in Guatemala. Your grandfather and my family are chosen to provide leadership for those poor indigenous people on the lands entrusted to us and make sure that they avoid making mistakes. They are truly our responsibility. You must always remember who you are and who they are. It is your sacred trust."

Granmama had etched that catechism into Leona's mind. And young Leona clung onto each of these words as expressions of affection by Granmama—how Leona craved the attention and affection of the Grand Dame, who in fact showed her little other warmth, except for an occasional pat on the head or a smile. Leona had wished for a warm embrace like those bestowed on her cousins, Maria Elena and Luis, the children of her Uncle Felipe, but she settled for the words that made her feel important.

Also Granmama made sure that Leona knew the history of her bloodlines. Her own family's participation with Coronado in the sixteenth century conquest of Guatemala and his reward from a grateful king. His family in Estremadura was already in the King's service and now this Conquistador was named a Conde in his own right and given land on the altiplano of Guatemala and all the people on that land to govern. "Yes", Granmama would say "you Leona are blessed to be of my blood."

She also told the little girl of her grandfather's family—noble but not as noble as hers. She described his family as impoverished in Estremadura with three sons whom the lands could not support. The father, a minor Conde, petitioned the King for a land grant in the New World and, as Granmama would disparagingly say 'no title,' just land that no one else seemed to want." And your ancestor, a mere teenager with his teenaged wife, the second daughter of an Asturian Conde, also of meager means, took several months on ships and wagons to reach Cuscatlán, a dependency of Guatemala and bestowed their blessings on the uncivilized indigenous people."

Granmama dismissed Leona's questions about her parents. She would tell Leona, "Your sweet mother lives in Paris and your father who visits you every Saturday is only a Greek merchant who by circumstance married into our family." How often had she been told that her father really didn't fit in as a member of her mother's family. "A mere merchant—a money lender!" Through her mother, not her father, she was born into two of the Great Families that had ruled Guatemala and El Salvador since the Conquest and their national existence. Granmama with condescension told her, "It is better for you not explore the merchant qualities and values of your father and his family—better left to imagination than trace the family tree."

Her grandfather dutifully echoed his

wife's massages and tone whenever he was around during one of the lectures. She seldom saw her grandfather except on family celebrations or working at the library. He usually had little patience for her. Only one time as a small child did she remember him other than impatient and cold. That day he summoned her to the library and reproved her for some misstep when she began to cry. He softened, smiled at her and told her, "You are not to cry. You are a Suarez Moncada."

When she dried her eyes, she quietly asked: "Grandfather why don't you ever tell me stories about the Suarez Moncada family. Granmama tells me many stories about her family in Guatemala and only a little bit about yours. She says I am of both your blood but I know so little about the Suarez Moncada."

Grandfather relaxed across the desk as he said, "I am so glad that you care. My ancestors came from a noble family in Estremadura. They fought alongside King Ferdinand in the Reconquista and were rewarded with title and land. In the middle of the eighteenth century, the family fell on bad times with the family fortune drained by the War of Spanish Succession and the hard economic times that followed. My ancestor, the Conde, implored the Crown for help. The King arranged for the marriage of the family's only daughter, an army appointment for the second son and a land grant in the New World for the third son, Felipe, a sixteen-year-old betrothed to Ana Maria, the second daughter of an Asturian Vicomte." These were details that Granmama had never included in her pronouncements.

"Felipe and Ana Maria had little more than letters from the Crown and the funds required for the passage from Spain to the New World. When they arrived in San Salvador, the provincial capital of Cuscatlán, they had little more than their wits and their first child. The land grant was not on flat land with many indigenous families living on them. They were sparsely settled, unproductive mountainous terrain. It was up to Felipe to find a way to make a livelihood from almost vertical production areas running up mountain sides from almost sea level to the sky. He organized the families on the land and introduced production of cacao and balsam as cash crops in addition to the traditional food crops. In that way he made some money and fed his household in San Salvador."

"My," said a surprised little girl Leona, "that is so different from the lavish lifestyle of Granmama's family in Guatemala, with great houses and hundreds of families working the fertile land for them."

Grandfather almost chortled as he continued, "Felipe made friends with the indigenous families on the grant and together they slowly increased production of crops and raised our and their family income, my family never earned enough to consider a return trip to Spain as Granmama's ancestors did periodically over the years."

"Despite her meager income from the land grant, Ana Maria and Felipe reared eight children and became leaders in the social life of the province," Leona's grandfather reminisced. "The eight children of Felipe and Ana Maria, your and my blood ancestors, not the land grant, were the foundation of today's family fortune. Eight children of noble blood and bearing were great catches for the rich and powerful in the Captain Generalship of Guatemala, of which Cuscatlán was a part of. The four sons were educated at the University of San Carlos in Antigua. The girls were trained by the nuns to read, write, and observe the proper social mores. Each of the eight children married into a leading Creole family of Guatemala and Cuscatlán—one daughter into the Arce family that led the movement for independence of Cuscatlán from Spain, Mexico and the first Central American confederation."

"Yes, it was my great, great grandmother Ana Maria who built the Suarez Moncada family. She lived well beyond her husband and quickly mastered the art of family decision-making. She learned the business side of running the land grant and made sure the family made a profit on each one of the transactions." His face almost glowed when he remarked, "Ana Maria mastered the political and economic landscape that moved the life of her adopted homeland and made sure that her children and grandchildren were always on the winning side. Yes, indeed, Ana Maria, the matriarch, created the power base of the Suarez Moncada family."

Grandfather paused and looked around the library at family pictures before wistfully continuing, "Ana Maria personally raised and incentivized my grandfather, her special grandson, the innovator who converted the family lands to coffee production and made them into some of the finest coffee plantations in Central America—the same fincas that currently feed the family's coffers. The innovator also induced his siblings and their families into the political partnerships that became the nucleus for the 14 families that have run this country for generations to this day." Grandfather boasted, "no decision has been made by the 14 without consulting the Suarez Moncada family."

Leona could almost hear him enumerate the presidents and generals in the family lineage and their role in ruling El Salvador over its first hundred years as an independent nation. He made no secret of his and the family's support for General

Martinez Hernandez and the dictatorship he created in 1931, nor of his pride in helping to overthrow the first liberal regime in the country's history, including the slaughter of indigenous communities whose only crime was that they supported the liberal regime and had demanded a greater voice in governing their own country. "Yes," he said, "The Suarez Moncada name was significant enough for your grandmother to marry me."

Leona never had another talk with her grandfather as she had that afternoon, but she was with Granmama often. Her imposing presence and manner etched into Leona's mind a message of her importance to the people on the fincas and her responsibility to be the mentor and to save them from making bad decisions. "Your family brought them civilization and redemption through the Church and Christ and civilization. You have to be prepared to make the decisions for them because they did not know how to take care of themselves. We, your family, brought the light to them and only we can keep it lit for them. We lead; they follow."

Granmama was always proper and stern with the little girl, almost no maternal warmth but she was the only constant female family figure in her young life. Neither of her grandparents ever mentioned either of her parents except to note that her father was the son of a Greek money lender—obviously not of the same lineage and caste of her mother. Her father visited her only on Saturday afternoons. Yes, he was loving and tender, but Granmama never spoke nicely to or of him. Her non-verbal messages confused Leona and left a question in her young mind: is he one of us or one of them?

When she was about four years old, she realized that Granmama made an annual trip to visit her mother in Paris. She was left alone in the mansion with a nanny. Her grandfather came by occasionally to work in the library. Her father never failed to visit her on Saturday afternoon. It was not until her teens that she began to understand the relations between her grandparents and parents in the real world beyond the Suarez Moncada mansion.

This confusion emerged from the shadows of her mind as she sought answers to her indecision and acquiescence at the afternoon meeting. She began to face the prejudices that had been sown so blatantly in her mind as a youngster. She realized for the first time that, even though her father had been the central feature in her education and business life, she had always carried doubts about his authenticity—was he one of us or one of them? She almost cried aloud, "Oh, Granmama, you really screwed me up".

Chapter 4

As she tossed in bed, trying to doze off, her mind would not relax. Leona found herself reliving her childhood in the mansion—and it was not a happy one much of the time. Oh, yes, she had all the material comforts, but the house was never filled with happy experiences or love. There were emotional barriers between Leona and her grandparents—seldom a kind word from either one. Granmama never embraced her or told her she was loved. Instead, Granmama would comment that Leona was not blessed with the fine Castilian features and light clear skin of her mother, but the swarthy roundish face of her Greek father. Granmama would often reprove her for lack of grace.

Grandfather was frequently away from the mansion and seemed to have little interest in her existence. She was there— little more. Only that one time when he told her of his family roots did he take much rime with her—she never remembered a time when he embraced her.

She could not remember a time when either of her grandparents had talked to her about her interests or needs. She sensed that her grandparents felt obligated to rear her, not to love her. She had seen them warmly react, even pick up and kiss, other grandchildren—but never her.

Nonetheless she craved their attention—especially affection from Granmama.

It was her own father every Saturday afternoon that rushed to hold her and lavish his attentions on her. He never arrived without a lovely present, and he focused only on her and her interests during those afternoons. Often Granmama sat across the room scowling at the scene before her—Granmama made no pretense of liking her son-in-law and, on every possible occasion would tell her granddaughter not to be deceived by her father's intentions.

Life in the mansion revolved around the protocols for discipline, manners, and actions that Granmama established. Under them, Leona was left to live in her bedroom and playroom. She could not remember a time that her grandparents were in her room. Maids took care of her, especially her Salvadorian nanny who woke her in the morning, bathed her and tended to her needs. Nanny told her stories and taught her how to read and write in Spanish. Nanny served her most of her meals that she ate either in her adjoining playroom or in a small dining alcove downstairs off the kitchen

Only on special occasions like family Saints' Days, family reunions or visits by cousins was she allowed to eat in the elegant dining room. Etched in her mind were the large crystal chandelier with its streaming prisms of sparkling light, the long formal mahogany table on which the French designed family silver was arrayed and the silver and crystal Old World platters, bowls and centerpieces that the family had acquired in antique shops and flea markets across Europe.

At those family occasions, she remembered how she sat at the children's table with her cousins and ignored them while she watched the joviality at the formal table and longed to be part of the aura of good feeling she felt emanating there—a feeling usually absent every day in the life of the mansion.

Two cousins were the only ones with which she seemed to be comfortable at those table. They were the children of her mother's only surviving sibling, Uncle Felipe. One was his daughter, Maria Elena; the other, his son Luis. They were her only primos hermanos (first cousins). Maria Elena always seemed to enjoy being with her—smiling, attentive, caring. They would play and laugh together, Luis, on the other hand, acted more like an older brother and treated both Maria Elena and Leona as they should obey him—but he seemed to notice them. So, unlike the others who treated her like a pest and made her feel out-of-place. She remembered how she particularly disliked her male cousins—except for Luis— who gulped down their food to get back outside where they would play football.

Maria Elena, was about Leona's age; and she loved to talk about her own life and told her all the special things she heard at home. Leona often didn't understand, but she loved to listen and ask questions, and Maria Elena seemed eager to share all she knew. The two would sit and talk and laugh until their nannies arrived to take them up to nap. Maria Elena was the only cousin Leona truly considered a friend.

The only other person that Leona considered her friend was Margarita, slightly older than she and the only young girl living in the mansion. She almost every day asked nanny to allow Margarita to play with her and go with her on walks through the patios and garden walkways of the mansion. That Margarita was the daughter of the cook never bothered her as it did Granmama. She tolerated the two girls playing together, but she repeatedly would scowl and warn Leona that Margarita was not one of us and could not be trusted. "You Leona must always remember who you are and who Margarita is, the cook's daughter."

Nonetheless, Leona looked at Margarita as an elder sister who helped her learn how to live in her complicated world. It was Margarita to whom she ran for solace after a disturbing session with her grandparents. It was Margarita to whom she turned when she felt uncared for and alone.

As she remembered that uneasy night, it was she Leona who always took from Margarita, seldom reaching out to her about her life, her thoughts, or her interests. She realized that frightful night that all her life she Leona presumed that only she mattered. Almost bewildered, she asked herself—for the first time she could recall-- what in that mansion had honed her to think only of herself?

Chapter 5

Leona turned over, trying to get some sleep, but instead was transported back to the party on her 5th birthday that Granmama held for her. All of the Suarez Moncada family was there, but not her father. She remembered Granmama welcomed her and admired the beautiful new lime green dress from Paris that her father had given her during his weekly visit the preceding Saturday. She remembered her Granmama patted and kissed her forehead. She remembered the warmth that filled her body. She remembered her grandfather toasting her birthday after which all the family stood up and smiled at her—even Granmama almost smiled. She almost felt the embrace of her prima hermana Maria Elena gave her that day and her words that the family was indeed grateful to Leona.

The following Saturday she told her

father about the party and how sorry he and her mother had not been present to share it with her. Granmama sitting across from them almost grimaced. Father then asked Granmama, "Is the dress available for Leona to show it off to me?" Granmama curtly replied," It is at the cleaners".

A few days later, Granmama called Leona and nanny to the Library and advised them, "I will be taking both of you in late April to Paris to visit Leona's mother, and the lime green dress is to be part of your wardrobe." Leona was overjoyed and rushed to Granmama, "Oh, I am so happy that you will be taking me to meet my mother and show her my birthday dress."

The news of the trip and the opportunity to meet her mother elated little Leona and she made all sort of plans about what her mother and she would do together. She imagined her mother's warm embrace when she burst into her house and how she and her mother would leisurely stroll, arm in arm, through parks and on the broad boulevards she saw in books that nanny brought up from the library.

The day finally arrived when Granmama, nanny and Leona boarded the IRCA train that took her on the two-day ride from San Salvador to the Puerto Barrios on Guatemala's Atlantic coast where they boarded a Great White Fleet banana boat for the voyage to New Orleans. On the seventh day of the adventure, they embarked on a French trans-Atlantic liner that took another week to carry them to France. Leona ignored any discomfort, inconvenience, or rough seas-- her anticipation was so overwhelming.

When they arrived in Paris, she eagerly looked out the window of the train, expecting her mother to be waiting for her. She was disappointed that her mother was not waiting at the Gare d'Nord. While nanny collected their steamer trunks and hand suitcases, Granmama arranged for a taxi to deliver them and their luggage to her mother's apartment. There was no sight of mother herself—and that perplexed the little girl.

A short taxi ride brought them to an elegant five story apartment building—with a doorman who assisted them to the elevator and welcomed back Granmama, reminding her that "Madame lives on the third floor. There are only two suites on that floor and her front door is to the left of the elevator."

A maid, not Leona's mother, opened the door and showed Granmama to a large airy room and Leona to a small one down the long hallway. The maid, an old family retainer from San Salvador, told Granmama in Spanish that mother was out making calls and should be home for dinner—and dinner would be at 8:00 PM.

After she was settled in her room, Leona decided to explore the apartment She found an elegant salon, a large dining room, four bedrooms, three baths and kitchen. Leona never found the room in which nanny and the maid stayed—she later learned that it was on the roof.

That evening set the tone for the four-week visit. Leona was served dinner in a small alcove off the kitchen and nanny put her to bed before mother returned home. She wept that night with disappointment. When she met her mother the next day, she was the beautiful elegant woman whose face Leona had seen in the framed photographs in the mansion, but her demeanor and reaction to Leona were a replica of Granmama—she made no effort to embrace her daughter and make her feel welcome.

The bodyguard jumped out of the car on the ready and with gun drawn as Leona waited for the long-time family chauffeur to open the door for her on her arrival home from the tumultuous private meeting of the country's most powerful families.

Oh, yes, indeed, mother did arrange for Leona to see the wonders of Paris, glide down the Seine in a bateau and walk along its broad banks, enjoy the Louvre, climb the steps of Sacre Coeur, attend mass at Notre Dame, visit Napoleon's Tomb and enjoy lunches at the Eiffel Tower and some of Paris' renowned cafes. Mother joined Leona and Granmama for a carriage ride through the Bois de Boulogne and several motor rides through the countryside. But, there was no warmth, It was like going through the motions of life as if they were in mansion in San Salvador. After that first night, she never wept again and wiped her mother from her dreams.

When they returned to the mansion, nanny helped Leona write a thank you letter to mother in Paris. Leona never received a reply.

The following year, 1939, before Leona turned 6, a tutor arrived—an English woman—Miss Pamela Jones. Granmama simply told her "Your father believes that, with war threatening in Europe, it will be best if you are educated at home. While I believe you would be well taken care of in a proper school in Switzerland as I was educated, your father insists that you remain in San Salvador. So, against my wishes, he has hired Miss Jones."

Nanny was sent to take care of cousin in Santa Ana, and Miss Jones moved into a room down the hall from the playroom. As it turned out, she became Leona's mentor, companion, and friend for the next six years while World War II raged in in Europe. Miss Jones educated Leona in reading, writing, arithmetic, history and geography. She taught her to speak and read English and

French as well as her native Spanish and introduced her to the great literature in the three languages. She brought science and world affairs into Leona's life. Her tutor became her friend and, despite protests from Granmama, allowed her other constant friend Margarita to share the classroom with her.

When Miss Jones entered her life in 1939, Leona felt for the first time that someone other than Margarita and Maria Elena truly cared for her. From the day of her arrival, Miss Jones focused all her attention on Leona, her interests and needs. She made education a wonderful adventure that opened up the world to that little girl. She offered the child a sanctuary where she would feel safe and affection even when Miss Jones felt it necessary to disciple her.

As these thoughts tumbled through her head, Leona had a revelation. For the first time she really absorbed Miss Jones' words that her father found and paid for Miss Jones—over Granmama's objections. She began to understand how her childhood obsession for approval and acceptance by Granmama had distorted her father's importance and role in her life. It was her father, not Granmama, that had been the primary positive force in her life. Why had it taken her so long to see how she undervalued his role in her life. She half sobbed, "Why had I not realized this before?"

Chapter 6

Leona was sitting up in bed almost seeing Miss Jones live across the room. She mellowed as she remembered how that lady became the center of her life as she was transformed from child to teenager. She realized how important Miss Jones had been in introducing her to the life around her and how caringly she made certain that she had a companion. Margarita, to share those years with her.

Shortly after Miss Jones arrived, Granmama called them to the library to inform them that she planned to take them to Paris to spend the month of May with Leona's mother. Granmama continued, "Miss Jones, once we settle in my daughter's apartment, you will be free to spend two weeks in Wales with your family. My daughter and I will see to Leona in your absence."

Miss Jones smiled and thanked Granmama for her consideration. Miss

Jones then suggested that they take advantage of Pan American Airways new flight to Miami, a train to New York and the deluxe llner Ile d'France from New York. Granmama bristled with the suggestion that she change the itinerary her family had used for decades, but finally agree to explore the feasibility when Miss Jones suggested, "It will take much less time to get to Paris and provide you with the most luxurious and comfortable facilities now available for your trip across the Atlantic."

It turned out that a suite was available on the Ile de France on Granmama's timetable, the time of travel was cut ten days and the cost was slightly less than Granmama had expected.

In the six weeks before they left the mansion, Miss Jones relived with Leona the sights she had experienced on her trip the year before and made them more wonderful than she had realized. She taught

Leona some elementary French and filled her head with the history and culture of France. Miss Jones so enriched Leona that, even with her disillusion about her mother, she excitedly looked forward to the trip.

When they reached Paris, mother once again did not meet the train and they took a taxi to her apartment. Miss Jones settled her in and spent the first night with her charge. The next morning before she left for Wales, she was introduced to mother by Granmama. Miss Jones nodded her head and said, "Delighted to meet you Señora Borakas"

Mother sharply responded, "Never address me by that name. I am Maria Concepcion Suarez Moncada—Madama Suarez Moncada."

In 1939 before World Wat II began. It was a repeat of the experiences of the year before. There was no coming together of mother and daughter.

Even to a six-year-old, Paris that year was a delight. Every place she visited she tried out the few words of French Miss Jones had taught her. Each site seemed to bring to life stories Miss jones had told her. The experience of riding around the right bank and walking on the left was filled with characters to whom Miss Jones had introduced her. Her enthusiasm even seemed contagious and the first time she felt a flow of admiration from mother and Granmama—and how she longed for their admiration and affection.

The last week in Paris Miss Jones was with her, and the two of them spent hours in the Louvre, walking hand in hand across the Ile de la Cite and the elegant parks on both sides of Seine. They rode city buses—even the Metro—to get around, Miss Jones always providing the site with an aura of wonder.

On leaving Paris in late May,

Granmama told them that mother was planning to move to Neuchatel (Switzerland) in the fall because of the threat of war that hung over Western Europe. Granmama said that she had contacted the nuns who ran the finishing school that she and mother, in turn, attended and they had found an apartment nearby that would become available in August and that mother had arranged to rent it.

Mother had barely left Paris when World War II broke out. She was safely installed close to the friendly nuns when Germany invaded Poland and the Allies declared a war that ravaged Europe for the next six years.

Back in the quiet of San Salvador, Miss Jones found herself cut off from seeing her family for those six years. The flow of letters brought her news of the trials and tribulations that her family faced, and she tried to bury her concerns by focusing on Leona and what she needed to do to provide her charge the education critical to a fruitful life. She lived and worked with Leona twelve months a year for those six years and covered the curriculum of the first eight years of public schools in the United Kingdom.

One area in which Miss Jones placed special attention was in language training. She guided Leona into becoming trilingual— English and French as well as her native Spanish. To assist her in French, she invited Granmama to come up to the classroom for tea and chats in French. Granmama like Leona's mother had spent six of her formative years at a Catholic girls' school in Neuchatel, and she was taught primarily in French, with course work in German and Italian that made her fluent in those languages as well. Granmama rejected the invitation at first but relented after Leona made a second request in flawless French.

For the next four and half years, Granmama came up to the classroom at least once a week to converse with her granddaughter. That delighted Leona even though her grandmother seldom became more affectionate than to commend her grammar and choice of words.

When Leona was eight, Miss Jones suggested to Granmama that Leona learn to swim and play tennis. Granmama accepted the suggestion and arranged for Leona to use the facilities of the Club de Golf, of which the Suarez Moncada had been founding members. Granmama also arranged for Leona's cousin, Maria Elena, to join Leona—as Granmama said, "It will be more economical for the family to pay for training both girls at the same time." Of course, the Club would not consider including Margarita, the illegitimate daughter of a cook, to use the Club's facilities.

So, twice a week Miss Jones took both youngsters to the Club for their lessons. This helped strengthen a lifelong bond between the cousins. While Leona had been sheltered in the mansion for most of her life, Maria Elena had been allowed much more freedom—she went to a private Catholic girl's school and was one of its most outgoing members. She learned everything about every other girl and her family. And she became the confidante of her mother who spent many nights alone at home while her husband apparently galivanted with his cronies and her older brother immersed himself in his interest in sports and his friends.

It was Maria Elena at the Club who told Leona about the family relationship with her father. One morning as the two girls were resting after a swimming lesson. Leona lamented, "I just don't understand why Granmama and my father never seem to get along. It makes me so sad. Like, on his visit last Saturday, he brought me a beautiful new blue jacket with gold embroidery. I was so happy until Granmama said that it was in poor taste— so typical of a money lender. Father seemed upset but I didn't know what to say."

The following Wednesday at the Club, the two girls were having a soft drink in the Club's dining room when Leona overheard two women at a nearby table referring to her "as the child of the agreement."

Leona whispered to Marie Elena, "What do they mean—child of the agreement?" Her cousin responded, "I am not sure, but I will ask my mother."

So Maria Elena pressed her mother that night for some information. Her mother not too reluctantly gave her an explanation that she shared with Leona at their visit to the Club.

Leona asked Maria Elena, "Did your mother tell you anything about the problems between Granmama and my father?"

Maria Elena said, "Yes, I talked to my mother and I'm not sure I understood everything. My mother told me that the Suarez Moncada family resents your father. It seems that the family ran into money problems. My mother added that, if her family in Guatemala had known about them, they would never have accepted Granmama's proposal for her to marry my father. She was a teenager when the families made the agreement for her to move to San Salvador and marry my father. After the marriage, she learned that the Suarez Moncada had lived in Europe in the 1920's and went into debt to cover their expenses. She told me never to borrow money from anyone.

"Well, the people who lent money to

grandfather was your father's family bank. The debt became so large that your father's family were about to take over all the Suarez Moncada's land and houses when grandfather and your father's father agreed on the marriage of your mother to your father— can you imagine, neither one had met the other. Granmama opposed the marriage but had to accept because otherwise the mansion and the fincas and all their treasures would be taken over by your father's family. She said that your father's family bought into Suarez Moncada family and that Granmama didn't like it."

Leona was thoroughly absorbed by the revelation and tried to absorb it. She said nothing except, "Maria Elena, I have so much to learn about my family and who I am."

After classes that afternoon, she and Margarita took a walk around the patios when Leona asked Margarita, "Do you know anything about why Granmama is always so mean to my father?"

Margarita asked, "What you mean?"

"Well, whenever my father visits me on Saturday afternoon, Granmama is always cross with him. I asked Maria Elena today, and she said her mother told her that is because the family got in debt with my father's family and his father made my mother marry his son. That's so confusing."

Margarita mused, "Leona, I don't know much about that. I've heard arguments between your grandparents that I didn't understand. They were all about spending too much money—your grandfather blamed Granmama and she blamed him. When they had money before the bad times began several years ago, they lived very well—a lot of time in Europe. When the bad times began, grandfather said that the debts kept growing. Each blames the other for what happened."

"When I asked my mother about it, she only could tell me that she heard Granmama accuse grandfather of making the arrangements for the marriage. My mother told me that she doesn't know much more, but she is sure that Granmama never approved and dislikes your father for having married her only daughter."

Leona remembered how perplexed she was as "the child of the agreement" and how this confusion had led her question the motives of her father and his family—and that she let it influence her feelings toward them even after she learned years later that it had been her grandfather who approached the Borakas family with a business proposition to allow his family to avoid bankruptcy, retain nominal control of the fincas and ownership of the mansion in return for the marriage of his daughter to the only son of the Señor Borakas.

Why was it only now that she Leona

was able to admit unequivocally to herself that 'the child of the agreement' was not because of a social climbing voracious money lender who exploited the Suarez Moncada family but because of an irresponsible family of spendthrifts that had sought the mercy of their creditors.

Chapter 7

During one of the weekly tea parties in the classroom with Granmama, Miss Jones suggested that she take Leona to the main family finca so that she could learn about coffee growing and life on the finca. Granmama was appalled at the idea of a female member of the Suarez Moncada family becoming engaged in the family business, "That is the work of men." Leona mentioned the idea to her father during his weekly visit as they walked through the Parque de Japon (later renamed the Parque Gran Britannia).

Somehow the following week, as they sipped their tea and ate their biscuits, Granmama reflected, "The world was changing—all too fast for my taste. The trip to Europe was much too rushed, taking a airplane to Miami hardly gave me time to plan my trip across the Atlantic—and the speed of the Ile De France—just four days from New York. I could hardly believe it. And all those chic ladies on board—many of them engaged in business. So unlike the days of my youth."

"Miss Jones, that set me to thinking about your proposal that Leona learn about the fincas, especially about Leona becoming too exposed to those people who live there and their evil ways. No matter how much we have tried to civilize them, they drink away their time and cause so much heartache to their benefactors like me. Well, I have decided that I will not object to taking Leona to the finca. Please take Margarita with you so that she can help you protect Leona while she is there."

Granmama looked away and then changed the subject to her daughter's new apartment in Neuchatel and the quiet life she was leading far away from the turmoil building in wartime Paris.

It took a week for Miss Jones to work

out arrangements for the visit with the housekeeper at the great house for a ten day stay. There was no telephone line, and she had to rely on the short -wave radio connection set up in the office of Leona' father to set a date and agree on accommodations and other details. She also talked to Margarita and her mother about what she should take for the visit. Granmama never interfered but she certainly was not enthused about the project. It was a great learning experience for Miss Jones because this was the first of a dozen visits to the finca she made with Leona and Margarita over the next six years.

Leona had been to the main finca several times with her grandparents at Christmas and Easter. Margarita had never been there before even though her mother had been born there to a family that for generations had been part of the Suarez Moncada workforce.

The route took them west on the Pan American Highway, the only modern paved highway in the country—part of the US sponsored project to link the Americas from Texas to Argentina and Chile. Halfway to Santa Ana, about two hours from their departure from the mansion, they turned off to the right and followed the Suarez Moncada property line, defined by barbed-wire fences covered in bougainvillea. They then maneuvered uphill on an unpaved lane, full of ruts created by oxen-drawn carts the country people used to tend their lands or go to market. It took nearly thirty minutes to reach the entrance to the sprawling one-story house built around the original adobe dwelling of Felipe and Ana Maria when they first came to occupy the land described in the original land grant from the King of Spain. Over the years the house had been enlarged and modernized with electricity, inside plumbing and other comforts but it retained its rustic essence.

Leona recalled Christmas and Easter at the house. Twice a year the family assembled for a ritual meeting with the farm tenants. The first Christmas she clearly remembered was when she was four. She visualized the corridors full of poinsettias and other Christmas laurels and the wonderful aroma that filled the house. She saw in her mind's eye the large dining room full of uncles, aunts and cousins—presided over by her grandfather and Granmama. Her grandfather's brother and sister and their spouses and children as well as her uncle Felipe, his wife and his two children. It was festive evening, full of wonder and a midnight mass celebrated in the great hall. She had never stayed up that late before.

On Christmas morning, Granmama sternly lectured her grandchildren, nieces and nephews of the importance of Christmas and their duties as hidalgos to the finca families: "These are sacred traditions that define our role in the lives of our tenants and reminds each of them who we are. We are the people who brought them Christ and civilization. It is we who bless them and provide the means for them to carry out their lives under the rules of the Church and our family. We are committed to treat them benignly and justly. So, act kindly but remember your place—and make clear they know their place."

On Christmas morning the family presided over the traditional greeting to the families who lived and worked full-time on the finca. The family was seated on the dais at the far end of the great hall, with Grandfather and Granmama in the center on large chairs. Leona sat at one end of the dais and her cousin Maria Elena at the other—the youngest members of the family.

Then, each finca family as a unit, one by one, was ushered into the great hall and her grandparents welcomed them by name.

Leona watched as each of the families in turn approached the dais, bowed to those on the dais and then received gifts from her grandparents—always the same—at Christmas, some household item for the parents, a ball for each boy and a doll for each girl. At Easter each family received a side of pork from the family farm just off the Pan American Highway.

Those formalities proclaimed that the Suarez Moncada were still Lords of the Manor.

As she tossed in bed, Leona especially remembered how different the trips with Miss Jones from those on Christmas and Easter. Her seventh birthday was celebrated during those ten days, and she met some interesting people with whom she interacted to the present day.

Leona, Margarita, and Miss Jones arrived at the finca in the early afternoon. After getting settled at the big house, Miss

Jones arranged for lunch in the dining room. She invited the foreman to join them. As he walked into the room, he introduced himself, "I am the foreman of the finca, Pedro Martinez—call me Pedro, everyone does. The patron has asked me to show you around the finca."

Miss Jones interjected, "I want you to do more than show us around the fincas. We want you to teach us all about coffee growing."

He smiled quizzically, Miss Jones responded, "Yes, Pedro, we want to learn about how the finca operates and would appreciate you making out a program. We will be here for ten days."

Pedro nodded his assent as he said, "We will start early tomorrow morning."

As he turned to leave, Miss Jones smilingly said, "Please join us for lunch." Pedro was clearly unprepared for the invitation. As far as he could remember, no patron had ever asked a foreman to sit in the dining room before. He awkwardly sat.

Miss Jones asked him about what they should wear. Pedro said, "Please don't dress up. Wear work clothes because I will show you each piece of our operations and let you participate if you want. I'll require you to get down on hands and knees and lots of physical exercise." Miss Jones asked Margarita and Leona how it sounded to them—and they were excited to have this new experience—a totally different routine than the school room at the mansion.

While they were talking, Leona watched the foremen, how he talked calmly but with authority and how much he seemed to know about his job. Yet she thought he was much younger than her grandfather or her father—not much older than some of her cousins. Leona asked him, "How long have you been foreman?"

He answered, "About three years. Mr. Borakas picked me. He sent me to the trade school run by the Fathers in Sonsonate and when I returned, I worked with him for about a year before he asked me if I was interested. I was surprised because I was born on the finca and none of the foremen I could remember had been from a finca family. They had been a friend of the patron."

Miss Jones asked him about himself and his education. "I graduated from the fourth grade at the village school across the road. My father had some books that your great grandfather gave him and one of them was a manual for taking care of machinery. I also read all the other books. You see, I, my parents and my grandparents were born on the finca. I was working as laborer when Mr. Borakas took over. He spent several weeks up here with us, watching us do our jobs. Then one day he asked four of us younger workers about ourselves and our plans, how much schooling we had and then started giving us more responsible jobs. He lent us some technical books to read and discussed them with us. He then sent all four of us to the technical school for six months. When we returned, he gave each of us important jobs. A few weeks later, he made me foremen and the other three—all good friends of mine—are my assistants who oversee each operation. You will meet the other three during your visit."

Leona seemed surprised and asked," My father took over the finca? I thought my grandfather was the patron."

"I'm not sure who is the patron, but Mr. Borakas is the person who comes here and tells us what to do."

After they finished eating, Pedro rose and said, "I still have some work to do before going home."

Leona liked Pedro. But hearing Granmama's voice in her head, she thought to herself that the foreman just didn't understand the importance of Suarez Moncada blood. Granmama had certainly made that clear to her that her father was just a merchant, with no head for more important things like running a finca. Leona could not accept then that the idea of training those young men came from her father, Mr. Borakas. The young Leona decided then and there that the decision to select Pedro had come from her grandfather, not her father, and that her grandfather ordered her father to act.

The first morning in work clothes the three ladies were introduced to the operations of the finca and the people who lived and worked there. The foreman showed them how the finca was laid out and the various steps in the process that transformed the cherries into coffee beans ready for roasting. He introduced them to his assistants who oversaw the planting and the four of them demonstrated how the land was prepared for planting and new bushes were planted, the amounts of fertilizer and insecticide the plant required and how it was applied. They took special care to explain the location and distribution of shade trees to offer the best chance for producing optimum amounts of high-quality mountain grown beans. Then they had the three ladies in turn plant a bush or two and monitor their work to make certain they had complied with finca standards.

For the next several days, the three ladies repeated the process in each of the coffee bean producing process. Pedro took them to mills, the drying yards and the other facilities where they worked with the assistant in charge, were explained what each operation included and then did the work. They got dirty and tired as they learned each operation and came to respect the ability and judgment of the foreman and his three assistants. Miss Jones summed it when she said to Pedro, "I am impressed with you and your assistants' knowledge of coffee growing and your ability to teach it to us."

Each afternoon after their work was over, the three ladies discussed what they had observed and learned and made a list of questions that they needed the foreman to answer for them. Leona also noted how different Pedro seemed from his assistants and the other workers. He was taller, with a much lighter complexion than his assistants and more articulate. The other three, especially Manuel, were impressive and competent, but Pedro just seemed different.

After cleaning up each day, Margarita and Leona would go out for walks around the finca, including the area in which the finca families lived. Margarita's mother had told her about the finca and the families who lived on it—after all her mother's family had roots there and she had been born there. So, it was special to Margarita to see for herself—and she wanted Leona to share this experience with her.

On the first afternoon, Leona and Margarita walked beyond the family garden to look at the houses of the foreman and assistants. There was no one else around while they walked around the four structures. Leona noticed that they were of adobe and recently white-washed, with red tile roofs. Through their windows they appeared to have three or four rooms—with discreet outhouses. The foreman's seemed slightly larger than the other three. Each had shade trees and small gardens surrounding them. They looked pretty much alike, nothing special about either one. As they were strolling, Margarita noted that the four-house appeared to be connected to the electrical and water systems of the big house. Leona wasn't impressed and said that she was tired and wanted to take a nap.

The next day they walked in the opposite direction for about half a kilometer until they reached the collection of about twenty-five houses in which the permanent finca families lived. They were all small, newly white-washed nondescript adobe buildings that appeared to have only a room or two, with small front yards in which corn, bean, peppers, and other food crops were planted. Most had one or two small windows and wooden front doors.

Leona seemed as unimpressed as she had been yesterday when she saw the foreman's and his assistants' houses and simply remarked, "I don't think the people like their houses. They don't do anything to make them pretty."

Margarita thought for a minute before answering, "My family has lived in one of these houses for generations. My mother was born in one of them. I hope to meet her relatives today or tomorrow and visit with them."

"Leona, they don't own or rent those houses. They are loaned to them by your family for only as long as they work on the finca. How they appear and how large they are depend on decisions by your family. And any improvements they might make belong to your family, not to the people who live there."

Leona's mouth fell open as she came to realize what Margarita had just told her. "You mean that my family could take the houses back and that the workers and their families would have nowhere to live. Is that also true of the houses we saw yesterday?"

Margarita merely nodded.

As they walked back to the big house, Leona was trying to absorb what she just learned: the power of the Suarez Moncado family over all over the people.

The following afternoon, the housekeeper accompanied the girls to Margarita's family adobe and introduced Margarita to her grandmothers and uncles. He grandmother embraced her warmly and looked at her tenderly. Leona looked on and recognized how different the skin tone and features of Margarita differed from those of her grandmother. Strange she thought: Margarita looks more like Granmama than her own grandmother. Her uncles also embraced her and their face and features were also very different.

The housekeeper had brought some bread and juice for the meeting and they sat in the sparsely furnished living-dining room with a straw mattress in one corner that indicated that it also served as someone's bedroom when nightfall came.

The family was very nice. The grandmother so caring and interested in all the news about the daughter she had not seen for several years and the granddaughter that was new to her life. Her uncles were not well educated but very polite and soft-spoken. They were not at all the kind of mean people that Granmama had led her to believe made up the finca families.

One of Margarita's uncles asked, "How is you mother doing? I miss her so much—she was my little baby sister. She was only 12 when the patron took her to San Salvador to take care of her after the terrible time she had. Does she like living in the city?"

Margarita replied. "Uncle, she has told me so much about you and she so loves you. I think that she is happy in the city, but she has told me many times that she misses all of you. You say she had a terrible time when she was 12. She has never talked about with me."

Her grandmother looked at her sons and the housekeeper. They seemed to agree not to say anything. They just looked blankly ahead. The housekeeper finally broke the silence, "Maybe it's time for us to go back to the house. Margarita, would you like to have your family join us for dinner one night before you go back to the city? Right now, I have to prepare for dinner tonight and must go back to the house. You girls stay a bit longer but remember to get home in time to clean up for dinner."

Once the housekeeper left, Margarita talked with her family about their lives, their families, and their children. Leona learned about the difficult times that Margarita's family had endured and how grateful they were to grandfather that they been allowed to continue living in the adobe after Margarita's grandfather died shortly before Margarita had been born.

Margarita said, "Dear grandmother, I

am afraid that we must leave for tonight. I will be back to see you tomorrow. And dear uncles, what pleasure it has been to meet you and to know how dear my mother is to you. I love you all." She warmly embraced each and then took Leona's hand to lead them back to the big house.

Every afternoon for the rest of the stay, Margarita visited her grandmother and uncles. The last night at the finca, she came home with tears in her eyes. Leona asked her "Why are you so sad?"

She replied, "Oh, I loved being with my grandmother and uncles and coming to know them and their lives. It has been very difficult for them since my grandfather died. My uncles worked as day laborers on the finca for several years and were paid little more than beans and tortillas. Now life is easier since your father pays all the families a better wage and lets them raise crops on the land around the house. And my mother sends them some money every month. Both of my uncles have their own families now and their wives help grandmother. Their lives are so different from mine in the mansion."

"I'm so sorry that your family has had such a difficult life. Let me help out," responded Leona. "I will ask my father to give her a better house and food."

Margarita embraced Leona.

Leona asked, "Did you find out about the terrible times of your mother?"

"Yes, I learned of the terrible time my mother suffered and why she was taken to the mansion. Please don't ask me more."

On the afternoons that Margarita was with her family, Miss Jones and Leona took their daily walk around the area where the family abodes stood. They came upon a new water well and small grove of young fruit trees -- mangos, papayas and banana stalks. At the well, they met several young girls around Leona's age filling ollas with water.

Leona said, "Buenas tardes, I am Leona Borakas." The girls seemed surprised that the daughter of the patron would open a conversation. They in turn said hello and gave their names.

Leona asked them, "How do you like living on the finca?"

The girls looked at each other before one shyly said, "Miss, life is not easy. But I suppose it is better than it was a few years ago. Now every day we go to school in town, and we have the new well so that we don't have to go down to the river for water."

Another chimed in, "My mother can do the washing at home instead of going down to the river."

Another said, "My family has lived on

the finca for many years, and grandma says that this is the first time the patron has put glass in the front windows.".

The fourth added, "We are eating fruit all the time now since the foreman planted the fruit trees— he said the fruit was for us to eat."

One of the girls added, "All of the leaks in our roofs are fixed and some of the houses now have tile floors instead of dirt."

The girls smiled and one by one they placed the ollas on their heads and warmly said gracias y hasta luego to their new friends.

When they returned to the big house, Leona said in a quite matter-of-fact voice, "I t want to know more about the life of the people here on the finca. I don't really understand how they live. I am sure pleased that grandfather is helping them to live better."

Miss Jones looked intently at Leona and said, "Young lady, it is Mr. Martinez who is making the improvements, and he works for your father. Don't you think that they should get the credit?"

Leona still heard Granmama saying," Your father is only a Greek merchant—what could he know about running a finca?" "No," she thought to herself, "Grandfather has to be telling my father what to do."

That Sunday the foreman Pedro Martinez escorted Miss Jones, Margarita and Leona to the little church in the community across the road from the main entrance to the finca. The town was a little more than a collection of adobe buildings on three unpaved streets. The main street had a small plaza around a *bodega* (grocery store), a *farmacia* (drug store), the *municipio y carcel* (municipal offices and jail), a *cantina* (saloon) and the *iglesia* (church). A few houses were painted, a few others white-washed but most were the dun brown natural color of adobe clay. There was an oil generator that provided electricity to the houses on the plaza and the plaza had a fountain from which the townspeople got most of their water. Of course, there was a cemetery not far from the church.

They went to church on a two-row buggy, drawn by two horses. The foreman's wife and their three children accompanied them. Leona noted that wife was a beautiful, graceful woman with warm green eyes and brown wavy hair. Her four-year-old daughter sat at her side. The other child was a boy about Leona's age crammed in at the edge of the front seat. Miss Jones, Margarita, and Leona occupied the canopy covered back seat.

Leona asked the boy his name. He said, "I'm Carlos Martinez." Leona asked, "Are you in school?" He replied, "I've have just the four grades in the village school and have received a scholarship from the Fathers in Sonsonate to go to school there." He looked backed at her as if to emphasize his good fortune. She found herself quite excited for him—and she felt some warm feeling she had not sensed before.

At church, he sat beside her and every chance they had they talked together. She asked where he would live in Sonsonate. He said that his father could not afford to have him live at the school but had arranged for him to live with a relative. Leona then asked Carlos, "What subjects have you studied at the school?" He said, "Pretty basic—reading, writing, arithmetic, some history and geography." They discovered that they shared a love of reading and geography. Somehow Carlos seemed like an old friend—in fact as she looked at him, he reminded her of her uncle Felipe, especially his eyes. She looked at him and she looked at Margarita—strangely she thought they both look more like a Suarez Moncada than she Leona did. Oh well, Carlos really made her feel very happy, and she hoped to see him again on her next visit to the finca.

When they returned to the big house, Leona asked Miss Jones about the school in the community across the road, and she agreed to make inquiries. The next night she told Leona that her great grandfather had sponsored the school, paid for its installation, and arranged for the teachers. "He built the convent and endowed it with money to pay the nuns for teaching there. All the finca children can complete the first four grades there without paying tuition because of your family's endowment. Children from the community, on the other hand, pay a fee each semester. Until your father came here a few years ago, few of the finca children went to school—now almost all do. The housekeeper told me that your father made another endowment for the nuns and encourages the finca families to educate their youngsters."

Leona just smiled and thanked Miss Jones. She thought again that it must have been grandfather who told her father to support the school. He was of the family that had done great deeds— what would a mere Greek merchant know of running a coffee finca with all those complex operations she had been learning about for more than a week.

So, when she returned to the mansion in San Salvador, she was eager to talk to her grandparents about what she had learned and what she had seen. In her weekly French conversation with Granmama she effusively told her all about her visit and the people she met. Granmama listened and nodded.

When Leona finished, she said merely, "How interesting. I spent most of my young life with the nuns in Neuchatel and only visited my family's finca on holy days. In my time, my father, brother, and uncles went to the finca, not we ladies. I suppose times have changed. Do be careful with the workers you meet there. They are not of our class, but they do need us to take care of them and, oh yes, lead them." She smiled at her granddaughter and began telling her of a dinner party she was invited to attend that night. Leona was confused, but she concluded that, since Granmama was such a great lady, it was with grandfather that she should share her finca visit.

A couple of days later, she spied grandfather working at the desk in the library and rushed in to share the details of her visit with him. He listened but did not comment. Only after she described the improvements to the houses of the finca families and the new well, did he respond with a solemn warning, "It is not wise to baby finca families. Do them one favor and they will expect more. Our role is let them know who in charge—not provide for all their comforts. Cover their necessities to insure they can keep working that's all a patron should do these days. If you give them special treatment or educate them at that village school, you will end up having to fight them. Mark my words! The workers are tough and ready to use machetes. We patrons must keep them under strict control."

On Saturday afternoon, when her father came to visit, he asked her about her visit to the finca, what she had learned, whom she had met and her reaction to the finca and the finca families, she gave some very general answers even when he encouraged her and spoke warmly of the qualities of the finca family—because deep down in her soul, the little girl kept hearing echoes of Granmama's demeaning words about her father, the Greek merchant.

That evening after the meeting, Leona remembered how confused she felt—not from her visit to the finca, but by the reactions of her grandparents. The "we" and "they" bothered her young mind very much. She had enjoyed her learning about the work and the life on the property. She admired Pedro and his ability to explain the growing process to her. She felt no animosity from the finca families and the warmth of Margarita's reunion with her family touched her deeply. Still the young Leona was looking at those experiences through the filter of "us" and "them" that Granmama had etched so carefully in her mind.

Chapter 8

Life in the mansion settled into a routine that lasted until the end of World War II. Leona's life revolved around the classroom, with Miss Jones presiding. Mondays through Fridays, except for Wednesday afternoon when Miss Jones took cousin Maria Elena and Leona to the Country Club for swimming lessons and Friday mornings at 11:00 AM when the parish priest gave Leona and Margarita lessons about their Catholic faith.

Thursday afternoon was special for Leona because Granmama, whenever she was in town, would come to the classroom for an elegant tea. Miss Jones would usually select a French classic for the three to discuss in French and Leona would glow for days whenever Granmama would praise her French or her analysis of the book. Leona would be so disappointed when Granmama was away from the mansion—and those absences were many since Granmama often spent months at a time at the home her family had given her in Antigua, Guatemala, when she married grandfather.

Every Saturday afternoon Leona spent with her father. He often took her out to lunch at his home or on a picnic to see the surrounding countryside, the lava black sands at the Pacific Ocean beach at La Libertad, the crater of El Bocaron or the nearby lakes Ilopango or Coatepeque. Every Saturday, her father brought her a present and listened as she told him about her week.

On Sundays several times a year, there would a family reunion—for someone's Saint Day, a holiday or special occasion. The Sunday festivities usually began about noon presided over by her grandfather and Granmama--and included grandfather's brothers and sisters and their families and her Uncle Felipe and his family—her father was never invited. It was only at these family gatherings that Leona saw her grandfather. Occasionally one of Granmama's family would visit from Guatemala and be the guest of honor.

Every Sunday morning when she was in town Granmama would take Leona to early morning Mass. Since Miss Jones was a Wesleyan, when Granmama was away, it was Margarita who accompanied Leona to church. Margarita never accompanied Granmama to church or participated at tea in the classroom.

Every Christmas and Easter, Leona accompanied her grandfather and Granmama to the principal fincas for the traditional greeting and homage. The script each year was the same, except that Uncle Felipe, his wife and two children were the only family members who participated. Leona wondered why grandfather's siblings and their families dropped out. It was many years later that she learned that they excluded themselves when their participation in the profits from the coffee trade had been curtailed by the terms of grandfather's agreement with the Borakas bank. Grandfather had protected only his own interests.

Miss Jones arranged two visits a year to the finca and made each visit an educational experience. To acquaint Leona with the physical and social character of her native land, Granmama's arranged visits to the homes of relatives or close family friends. Before reaching her tenth birthday, Leona had visited all of the ten Departments of El Salvador, been to the borders with Guatemala and Honduras and made two visits to Grandamama in her elegant colonial home in Antigua. Other than those short absences, all World War II years was spent at the mansion and on the routine that Miss Jones established and enforced.

CHAPTER 9

Several weeks after the first visit to the finca, on a Wednesday afternoon, Miss Jones took Leona and her cousin Maria Elena to the Country Club for their weekly swimming lesson. After the lesson and the girls had dried off in the afternoon sun, Miss Jones ordered their afternoon tea. They were talking happily when they heard two ladies at a nearby table talking about Maria Elena's father.

In an almost muffled but clearly understandable tone, one of the ladies said, "Did you hear about the family problems of Felipe Suarez Moncada?"

"No". replied the other. "I always thought the family was so careful after the troubles at the finca."

"Well, that's not what I hear. My cousin told me that his wife threw Felipe out of the house for having an affair with some low-class woman."

Leona looked quizzically at her cousin and Miss Jones. Maria Elena started to cry. "There, there," said Miss Jones as she hurried the girls to the family limousine.

In the car all the way to the mansion, Maria Elena sobbed. Miss Jones tried to reassure her while Leona continued to be confused. They quickly went up to the classroom on the second floor—the private area in which Leona and Maria Elena had many happy hours. Before it had always been Maria Elena the happy know-it-all who regaled Leona with amusing stories of life beyond the mansion.

Today it was Maria Elena who blurted out. "I am so unhappy. I so love my mother and father. I get so upset when they fight and that lady was right. My mother and father have been screaming at each other night after night, accusing each other of all sorts of things. One night, I heard my mother accusing him of wasting her inheritance on gambling, drinking and another woman. She screamed, 'You are just like your father. I have had enough. I've told my family to take action to protect my financial interests and get you out of my life. Get out of this house right now'. He left the house and hasn't come back."

Maria Elena was crying profusely. Leona tried to comfort her cousin. Miss Jones, in her stiff-upper-lip Welsh manner also tried to reassure Maria Elena that it would work out well. Leona was not sure what it all meant and was too concerned for her cousin to ask—indeed she asked herself, "Who can I ask to explain what it all means. I can't ask Granmama because of grandfather. I doubt that Miss Jones or my father knows secrets about Maria Elena's parents and my grandparents. I'll have to ask Margarita what it all means."

It must have been another hour

before Maria Elena was sufficiently composed to be taken home and face her mother.

Late that afternoon, after schooling was done and Miss Jones had retired to her room, Leona turned to Margarita and told her what had happened at the Country Club.

Margarita chose her words very carefully because she knew how innocent and protected Leona was. Margarita knew that Leona had never been told much about the workings of the household in which she lived or the family of which she was a member—and that her answer had to be carefully stated. Through her own and the other servants, she heard most of the gossip about the Suarez Moncada household, but instinctively Margarita never discussed those nooks and crannies with Leona or Miss Jones. Now faced with a direct question, she weighed carefully how much could she share them with Leona. Well, she would tell her now as much as Leona needed to know.

Margarita began, "Felipe has always been my mother's favorite and they have a special understanding since they were little children at the finca. When she was little girl, Felipe and one of her older brothers were friends and she would follow them everywhere. Felipe was always nicer to her than her brother who called her the little pest. They just grew up liking each other."

"Mother tells me after she came to the mansion, whenever Felipe had a personal problem, he would talk it out with her—as if she were a special friend. While I really don't understand what happened between Maria Elena's parents, my mother tells me that it was over someone Felipe has loved for many years—someone at the finca. It is over that girl that they have fought for many years. "

"Well, I know that Felipe has been living in his old room downstairs for a few weeks. We often hear Granmama insisting that he return to his wife and family. Mother told me that Granmama arranged Felipe's marriage to the daughter of a close Guatemalan friend after the family prevented him from marrying the girl he loved at the finca. We met her. She is Mrs. Martinez, the wife of Pedro and mother of Carlos. My mother told me last night that Felipe has always loved Carlos' mother, not his wife and that his wife found out."

Margarita added, "Felipe is living here, but your grandfather is not. Granmama for appearances allows him to preside over family events and use the library whenever he has business to take care of, but they are barely on speaking terms. This problem is not new, but it has become bitter. Grandfather is now living nearby with another lady and their children. My mother thinks there are three- one of whom is older than your mother. I heard that he is very happy living there and loves the lady. My mother tells me that Granmama has refused to allow him to separate from his vows to her. You should know because you may well hear people speaking about it as Maria Elena did today."

Leona stared at Margarita—a total lack of words. It was a shock that led her to ask herself questions about her family. Why does my mother live in Paris? Why did my father—not Granmama—hire Miss Jones? Why did she see her father only on Saturdays? Why did she live at the mansion, not at her father's house? And, above all, what should be her relationship with the various members of her family? Leona the little girl did not ask those questions—only let them churn inside her head. She reassured herself that Granmama would explain all these confusing matters at the right time. For now, she tried to understand Maria Elena's problem and Uncle Felipe's.

Margarita recognized what a shock her words had been to the eight-year-old. But it was better that Leona heard them from Margarita in the classroom than by surprise outside the mansion as had Maria Elena at the Country Club. Margarita put her arm around Leona's shoulders to let her know that she Margarita was there whenever Leona needed her. She half whispered to Leona, "I truly hope that these problems will blow over. Many married couples have problems and then come back together."

Leona hugged Margarita. "Thank you for explaining all that to me. I don't really understand what it all means because I have never seen my mother and father together."

A few days later, Margarita advised Leona, "Felipe told my mother that he would not be returning to his home. He gave it to this wife and swore to her that, despite the rumors, he had never been unfaithful or gambled. But, he told his wife that he could no longer pretend and make life miserable for all his family. He confessed that he still loves Carlos's mother and Carlos as much their children. He has moved back into the mansion and plans to stay."

Margarita paused and looked at Leona before continuing, "You don't really understand what I am talking about, do you Leona?"

"I am not sure what unfaithful mean," she replied.

"You really know nothing of relations between a man and a woman; do you?"

Leona's reply was a quizzical look.

"Well, I am not the one who should tell you. It should be your mother or Granmama. No, you should ask Miss Jones—she is your tutor."

Margarita realized that she may have said too much to the sheltered eight-year-old, but she added, "I will tell Miss Jones what I told you and tell her that you didn't understand what unfaithful means." She then hurried back downstairs.

A day or two later, sitting at tea, Miss Jones said reassuringly to Leona, "Margarita has told me about your question to her and her answer to you. I agree with Margarita that she had to give you an honest answer. It was hard on Margarita to tell you about your grandfather and uncle. So, if you have any further questions, please ask me. I don't know as much about your family as Margarita and her mother, but I am here to help you grow up as much to be your academic teacher."

"Well, I guess that Maria Elena's family is breaking apart like mine—all because of something Uncle Felipe and grandfather have done. I don't know what unfaithful means but I guess it's pretty bad," responded Leona.

Miss Jones looked intently at her charge before replying, "Unfaithful means that a husband or a wife has fallen in love with someone other than the person to whom he or she is married to. It is a sin, but it happens all too often. Two people stop loving each other."

Leona looked intently at Miss Jones and asked, "Is that what happened to my mother and father?"

Miss Jones responded, "I don't know what happened between your mother and father, but I promise to tell you when I find out. I do know that Uncle Felipe has moved back into the mansion and occupies the bedroom across the hall from Granmama's. He lives here now and your grandfather does not. I also know personally why Maria Elena's mother won't let him live at their home. I have heard rumors that it is your

Uncle Felipe's fault, but I don't know why."

"The most important thing right now is that you understand that you are in no way personally involved. The problems were caused by other people. Just accept that they occurred. The most you and I can do is help Maria Elena deal with the separation of her parents."

Leona just looked at Miss Jones as she absorbed her words. But they made her uncomfortable deep inside—her sense of security was shaken. For the first time she could remember, she felt threatened by a world beyond her secluded area in the mansion. She realized that people could hurt each other more than by a push or nasty words. She felt that somehow, she had to protect herself from that world—that she was the only one who could really protect herself.

Miss Jones asked, "Are you all right?"

"Yes, I guess so. It's so much to understand."

The next Saturday, Granmama was away from the mansion when Mr. Borakas arrived to visit with his daughter Miss Jones accompanied Leona to library. Father embraced his daughter and said, My love. Are you ready to come to my house for lunch today?" Leona smiled a yes.

Miss Jones interjected, "Mr. Borakas, Leona had a disquieting experience at the Country Club." She described the gossip, the impact on Maria Elena, Leona's question to Margarita and Margarita's response. She continued, "I told Leona yesterday that if she has questions, please share them with me. Although I don't know the family history that well, I believe that it will be easier on Leona if she confided in me."

Mr. Borakas seemed a bit surprised, "I had not expected my little girl would grow up so quickly. Yes, Miss Jones, I would welcome Leona sharing her concerns with you. And, please allow me to help answer those concerns whenever you deem it appropriate."

Leona gulped, almost embarrassed. She remembered thinking to herself, what would the Greek merchant know about the inner workings of Suarez Moncada family. It is Granmama whom Miss Jones should consult.

Chapter 10

Half-awake Leona could hardly realize that she was reliving a part of her life that she had carefully filed away. What in that image in the mirror forced her to reopen this facet of her life? Then, she said to herself that she should stop remembering and get some sleep after yesterday's harrowing meeting. The more she tried to convince herself, the more the remembrances of the years at the mansion swept over her. She was clearly seeing her classroom and going through the routine in which she lived for over six years.

Those were the years of war—first, in Europe and then the whole world. During those war years, information in San Salvador was very limited. Daily newspaper rarely had much news coverage beyond the official communiques of governments. Radio reception was primitive and blurred by static. Miss Jones every morning began classes with an update on the battles going on in Europe and later the Pacific—she tried to blend history, geography, and political science for Leona and Margarita—and occasionally Maria Elena.

Life at the mansion became livelier after Uncle Felipe, moved back in. While Leona saw or knew little about his comings or goings, the house didn't seem as empty. And, every Sunday Granmama had family lunch in the dining room—with Uncle Felipe, Maria Elena, her brother Luis. Miss Jones and Leona—she never invited Mr. Borakas or grandfather. Those meals were often filled with happiness since they were the one time each week that Maria Elena and her brother shared with their father and they saw each other lovingly what had happened to each of them during the week. They even let Leona contribute. Granmama just listened, sometimes with a slight smile lighting up her usual stoic face.

Those Sundays became weekly events that Leona looked forward to. Her Uncle made her part of his family—the first member of the Suarez Moncada clan who ever let her completely feel truly welcome. He smiled and he laughed, and he seemed to like people. Whatever had happened between Maria Elena's mother and him never came to the Sunday dinner table.

One Sunday, after lunch Uncle Felipe, Maria Elena and Leona sat in the library chatting about some events of the past week. Quite by chance Leona saw two black-framed photographs of two young men. She had never noticed them before. She asked Uncle Felipe, "Do you know those boys?"

He said deliberately, "Yes, those are my older brothers, your uncles, who died before either of you were born."

Maria Elena asked, "Are they the ones who died in accidents at the finca?"

"Yes", he replied. "Arturo was the oldest son. He was a wild one. The other is Guillermo who loved to ride motorcycles. I was very young when they were killed. Arturo got into a fight and a machete attack got him. Guillermo drove too fast over the road to the finca and ran into a tree. Arturo was Granmama's favorite and she grieved for years. I was the third son so different from my brothers. Well, that's enough. Let's get back to what your girls plan to do next week."

Leona then ten-years old asked herself, "Why didn't anyone tell me about those uncles? What's this big family secret?"

Back in the classroom Monday morning, she asked Miss Jones and Margarita, "Did you know I had two uncles who died before I was born?"

Miss Jones, quite surprised at the question, said, "No."

Margarita looked intently at Leona and said," You mean your uncles Arturo and Guillermo. Yes. I have known of them all my life. How do you learn of them?"

"The black-framed pictures in the library," replied Leona. "Can you tell me anything about them."

Miss Jones interjected, "This is school time. You girls can talk about them after school."

Once school was over, Margarita said to Leona, "The two were not nice men. They were spoiled and willful—so unlike Felipe and you. Granmama believed they could do no wrong. But they did. Please don't ask me anymore. I think Felipe or you father should tell you about them." Almost sobbing Margarita ran out.

Leona noted that Uncle Felipe had changed the subject Sunday and really didn't want to discuss his late brothers. So, she thought she would ask Granmama at their tea next Thursday.

Then, Miss Jones re-entered the classroom, "Where's Margarita?"

Leona simply said, "She went downstairs."

"Well, no problem, because I really want to talk to you about this book by Gide which I thought we could discuss with Granmama at tea on Thursday."

As she remembered that Thursday afternoon, she could almost hear Granmama's plaint in French as she looked at one of textbook in English, "You should be studying German, not English. It will be more useful when you go to Neuchatel for college and after all French and German are so much more colorful languages than English. But your father insists that you learn English and he is unable to understand his own bad judgment. Ah, yes dear, we must comply with your father's wishes, but always remember he is Greek, not a Suárez Moncada."

She recalled how Granmama used those French conversations to deepen Leona's acquaintance with her family, both her fraternal and maternal ancestors. "Ah", the older lady would repeat regularly, "My bloodline runs to the nobles of Spain—so much closer to royalty than those of the Suárez Moncada clan. You are so fortunate to be part of this blood-- with such fine land in Spain, Guatemala, and El Salvador. O, Leona, I wish you could have been at my elegant wedding in the cathedral of Antigua when the cream, of Central America came to celebrate my marriage to the dashing oldest son of the Suarez Moncada coffee empire. What a strategic alliance we formed".

That gave Leona the opening to report, "Granmama I saw those two black-frame photos in the library Sunday and was told that they were my late uncles Arturo and Guillermo. Please tell me about them."

"Ah", almost on the verge of tears, Grandame sighed, "What a beautiful pair of sons. Arturo was conceived on our six-month honeymoon in Europe. When I got pregnant, we returned to the mansion in San Salvador to await his birth—and what an exceptional lad. He grew to almost two meters, blond hair, blue-eyed—so like my side of the family. He could do everything and was so smart. He was the most handsome, virile young man you can imagine—and he loved the girls, and they loved him. I never thought that he would die. He was barely 20. The innocent victim of a malicious machete by drunks at the finca."

"I thought I could never stop weeping. I still had your uncle Guillermo to console me—only two years younger than

Arturo. So virile and almost as handsome. He loved sports and his motorcycle. I was devastated when he was killed near the finca in that horrible accident when he was only 19. Since his death, I have only gone back to that finca for the traditional Easter and Christmas *droit d'seigneur* ceremonies—to show them that we remain in charge despite our terrible losses."

"What terrible vacuums they have left in my heart. Oh, yes, in later years your Uncle Felipe and you mother became my solace, but they just never had the flair and charm of Arturo and Guillermo, Yes, I love my Felipe and Maria Concepcion, but life would have been so much richer if Arturo and Guillermo were still here to embrace me." Leona could see the glisten of the tears on her Granmama's cheeks.

Granmama then said, "Another tragedy has been Felipe and his failed marriage. Oh, how hard I worked to arrange his betrothal to one of my dearest childhood friends from such a famous Guatemalan family. Felipe never seemed to have the talents of his older brothers and some very peculiar fixations. He was indeed as handsome as his brothers—yes, all my children had the refined features and elegance of their ancestors, but Felipe I just cannot understand."

"Now, my Maria Concepcion was a beautiful child and I arranged for her to be educated by my dear Sisters at Neuchatel and meet the sons of some of my closest childhood friends. They all loved her, and I had such high hopes for her future. Grandfather and I visited her twice a year and took her with us on our vacations. She loved Paris and Florence and our visits to the art galleries, palaces, and cathedrals. I had such great plans for her marriage into one of the great families of Guatemala when circumstances forced her marriage to your father."

After a brief pause, she continued, "Isn't it time to discuss Gide?" She almost deliberately changed the subject when the marriage of Leona's parents came up in conversation.

On Saturday, when she lunched with her father, she asked him, "Did you ever know my uncles Arturo and Guillermo?"

"No," said her father. "They had both died before I met the Suarez Moncada family. I only know of them through the eyes of people who knew them."

"I saw their pictures in the library Sunday and Uncle Felipe told who they were but not much about them. Then at our Thursday tea, Granmama told me about them—handsome, talented young men who were killed in accidents at the finca."

"There are many finca families that remember them as troublemakers. Several have talked with me, but I have no personal knowledge or experience with them. The family member other than your Granmama and grandfather who really lived with them is Uncle Felipe. He was their younger brother. I think that he must have been about fifteen years old when Arturo was killed and seventeen when Guillermo died in the motorcycle accident. Would you like to talk to him about his brothers?"

"Yes", Leona said. "It was Uncle Felipe who identified the pictures last Sunday, but he didn't tell Maria Elena and me much about his brothers!"

"Do you want me to ask him to talk to you again?"

"Please, father, do."

Several days later Uncle Felipe came up to the classroom about teatime. He knocked on the door and called to Miss Jones, "May I come in and join you for tea today. Leona's father suggested that I might help her come to know my brothers Arturo and Guillermo whose pictures she saw in the library."

"Of course," Miss Jones replied.

As he came into the classroom, he said, "Please finish your class. I'll just listen." He sat on a chair near Margarita until they completed their analysis of a book by George Eliot." You know I have never studied English literature. There were no courses at my parochial school here or in law school at Salamanca. Perhaps Miss Jones, you can introduce me to some English classics I should read."

"Why, yes, yes," Miss Jones replied. "You know Maria Elena is often the third member of our class on English and French literature."

Margarita arranged for the tea to be brought to the classroom, and then she excused herself. "I promised my mother to help her on some chores this afternoon". Margarita sensed that the discussion would be about Leona's late uncles, and she was not uncomfortable being a listener.

They drank their tea and talked about the weather and the War. Until Uncle Felipe said, "I have never wanted to talk about my brothers. I was the youngest and they bullied me. Made fun of me. But they were my brothers, and my parents idolized them. So, I never wanted to complain—just go along."

"But, Granmama told me they were so handsome and talented," interjected Leona.

"Oh, yes, they were very smart and so handsome. Blond, blue-eyed Castilian noble features—they almost looked like angels in a Boccaccio painting I saw at the Vatican. But they both had nasty streaks. And those streaks got them into trouble."

Miss Jones looked a bit embarrassed and said, "I think you would be more comfortable, Mr. Suarez Moncada if I let Leona and you talk privately about this family matter. So please excuse me." With a smile, she rose and left the room.

"Uncle Felipe, I did not mean to upset you. You have been so kind to tell me of the hurt that caused you. I don't need to know any more now."

He embraced Leona and said, "You are a dear child. I am so glad you are Maria Elena's closest friend." He rose and left Leona alone in the classroom.

As she tossed in her bed, Leona remembered how she still looked forward to her weekly teas with Granmama and how she would glow when Granmama said anything favorable about her—whether it was her ability to speak French, the new dress that her father had given her, her astuteness or her growing up. Then, Leona remembered that never once did the older lady ever embrace her or smile at her as she did with her cousin Maria Elena.

CHAPTER 11

Leona yearned to sleep, but she kept remembered things that she had quietly tucked away for years. Each recollection revived another. The camera in her mind kept brining new images of those years in the mansion and the trips to the finca, especially those related to the men in the picture frames draped in black. Arturo and Guillermo were the handsome young men whom Granmama adored and Uncle Felipe abhorred. Until now, she had let Granmama's vision of her sons prevail. And now she was beginning to realize that her childhood thirst for Granmama's approval had skewed her thinking about so many important corners of her life.

She began reassessing various experiences and comments about her uncles Arturo and Guillermo. She was carried back to the ten-day visit that her ten-year old self, Miss Jones and Margarita made to the finca a few weeks after she first spotted the black draped frames in the library.

She saw herself walking with the foreman Pedro Martinez, hectare after hectare, inspecting new plantings, improved fertilizer techniques and changes in the drying area. He was explaining to her why the changes were made and the increased productivity per hectare he expected. These had been his initiatives and had earned him a substantial bonus—which he shared with his three assistants.

She could see the faces of Pedro and his three assistants and could almost hear their words as they deepened her knowledge of fincas operations. She visualized the layout of the coffee bushes and the trees protecting them from the scorching sun. They were sitting on newly installed benches near the water well and orchard discussing suggestions for improving the packaging of the coffee beans. Miss Jones and Leona asked some questions about the proposals and their costs.

For some reason Leona remembered that one of the assistants compared their proposals to the practices in the old days and commented, "When I was a little boy, I rode on oxcarts filled with bags of coffee beans bound for the Sonsonate warehouses for further packaging before they went to Acajutla for shipment abroad. Now we are planning to do all the packaging here on the finca."

Leona said, "How many years ago are you talking about?"

The assistant replied, "Maybe ten or twelve years ago."

"You must have known my uncles Arturo, Guillermo, and Felipe then."

A deep silence as they looked one to

another.

The foreman Pedro said, "I guess all of us had experiences with them…. Getting back to the packaging."

"Yes," said Miss Jones. "Let's hear more of your plans."

Leona noticed how Margarita was upset, and she kept her next question in her mouth.

When they returned to the great house, Miss Jones quietly said to Leona that she should not discuss her uncles at the finca, "They are very controversial personalities to the finca families. When I saw how interested you were in your dead uncles, I talked to your Uncle Felipe and your father. Uncle Felipe told some very delicate information that he felt you were too young to understand. But your question this morning leaves me no option. You do need to know more about those two men so that you do not unwittingly open old wounds. I hope you understand, Leona."

The little girl was very confused—she believed what Granmama had told her. She was surprised that her innocent question had caused discomfort to anyone. Leona thought that, since she had me come to know almost all the twenty-five finca families, they would know that she did not mean to be hurtful. She had laughed with them and even cried when someone had a problem—and she always tried to help. She even convinced her father to let her invite finca children about her age to afternoon tea. How could anyone believe that she would do anything to cause them problems. How could Miss Jones believe that she Leona would do anything to tell her anything prejudice those relationships.

But as she trusted Miss Jones, she agreed to ask no more questions about her uncles.

It was two nights later after dinner, that the housekeeper joined Miss Jones, Margarita and Leona in the dining room. She was quite upset as she spoke, "Excuse me for bothering you. But I must tell you that several people have told me their concern about Leona's asking about her uncles Arturo and Guillermo. Some believe that the patron plans to punish them for what happened all those years ago."

"I don't' think any of you know what life on the finca was like when they were alive. Please Miss Leona do not mention them again while you are here."

Miss Jones reassured the housekeeper, But, Leona said, "I don't understand why you are scolding me. I did nothing wrong. I can't believe that any of the finca families could imagine that I wanted to hurt them by asking that question."

Looking at Leona, Miss jones said, "It

is much more complicated Leona. You may not have intended any harm, but you opened up a matter that was buried years ago. So, I will tell you some of the information Uncle Felipe shared with me. Please just listen carefully to me."

"You remember a few weeks ago when Father Gallegos talked to you about sins and what actions you should not do. You remember about his telling you not to have sexual relations until you are married, and you asked me what the father meant. I showed you the anatomical pictures of men and women and tried to explain how one had sex. I saw how surprised you were since we have lived a very sheltered life in the schoolroom. Well, the problems with your uncles causes have a lot to do with their sinful sexual relations with daughters of finca families."

Margarita looked at Miss Jones and started to get up to leave. Miss Jones asked,

"Please stay. I know this may be painful." Margarita nodded and sat back down.

Miss Jones continued, "Well not all the people observe the teachings of the Church not to have sexual relations until one is married. A lot of young people get urges to be with another person, hold them, kiss them and then commit the sin. On the finca, the patron and his sons, from the time of your ancestor Felipe, have engaged in sex with the young ladies of the finca families. That is why you often see a member of a finca family resemble your grandfather or one your uncles. Yes, Leona, many share your blood. Some of the sexual relationships have been voluntary—love affairs that didn't last very long."

The housekeeper interjected," Oh those Suarez Moncada men were so handsome and virile. Sometimes we girls competed to have them make love with us—even though our fathers were usually furious. Sometimes the men forced themselves on us and we gave in—that often brought out the machetes and fights. Miss Leona, you have no idea how dashing your grandfather was," she caught herself and stopped speaking.

Miss Jones tried to conceal a smile as she continued, "Your uncles Arturo and Guillermo were not nice men. They imposed themselves on everyone. They were almost a head taller than the finca boys their age, and they pushed them around and beat up on them. They took any girl they wanted—no matter her or her family's resistance. Then one night Arturo took by force a twelve-year old girl—one not much older you- and beat her for resisting. That is called rape."

Miss Jones seemed very uncomfortable as she looked intently at Leona to see if the ten-year old was absorbing her words. The little girl's family was enraged. Word spread through the finca community and Arturo, grandfather and Granmama were besieged by the community. The family could not leave the great house and had to call for Army protection. There were several nights of fights and shootings. The father and neighbors of the little girl got drunk in town at the cantina and when on their way back to the finca, they met Arturo and Guillermo, who sneaked out of the great house, drinking with a couple of rowdy teenagers from town. They cornered him and hacked him to death. The girl's father was also killed—by a gunshot from Guillermo. Several other finca men were injured. Your grandparents fled from the finca with the other three children after General Martinez sent a detachment to settle the finca down."

"Many people were injured in the fighting. Several were arrested. When it was quiet again, your grandfather met with the family of the little girl, agreed to let the widow and her children continue to live on the finca and made special arrangements for the girl whom Arturo raped."

The housekeeper said almost involuntarily, "Well, after all, Arturo was his mother's favorite but so ungallant as his father used to."

Leona noticed that Margarita twitched, and her eyes were filled with tears. She also noticed for the first time how much the darker-skinned Margarita resembled the face in the black-draped photograph in the library. The ten-year old hadn't put all the pieces together, but she wondered if Margarita is part of this terrible event.

Miss Jones was visibly upset by the housekeeper's interruption and hastened to finish her explanation. "Oh, yes, I was also told that Guillermo came back regularly to the finca, kept pushing his weight around and went right on riding his motorcycle whenever he came to the finca. He ran over, knocked down and injured finca family members. So, when he had his accident, no one went for help until it was too late to save his life."

Leona was shocked. She couldn't believe people could be that cruel to each other, and certainly no one of her noble family could be so mean, especially to the finca families she had come to know. She felt very sorry for the finca families and especially the little girl. She also grieved for Granmama who lost her two handsome sons and thought to herself, why hadn't grandfather taught them to treat the finca families better. She looked at Miss Jones and said, "That is a very sad story. I won't mention my uncles again."

As the remembrance of that incident sank in, Leona broke out of her dreamy state and turned on the light. "Oh my God, until this very minute I have felt sorry for Granmama because of those two uncles. I saw her as their victim—as much as the people they hurt. Why was I so blind to her spoiling them and looking the other way? Why did it take this afternoon and looking into the mirror to accept the truth?"

"And why has it taken all these years for me to admit to myself that margarita's mother was the twelve-year old rape victim and Margarita is the child of that rape. How can I make it up to Margarita?"

CHAPTER 12

Leona was now clearly transfixed. How blind she been to reality. She was chiding herself for ignoring the obvious and letting her obsession about Granmama color her perceptions. She had thought herself so educated and informed that she could handle just about any situation by herself. Just as she had felt up to the meeting that afternoon. She was now looking at herself no longer as an infallible woman.

With a new sense of reality about her own limitations, she renewed her search for some reason for her inaction at Luis's meeting. Her mind's eye jolted her back to the classroom when Miss Jones was leading her from childhood to being a young lady. She saw Miss Jones seated in the classroom introducing Margarita and her to not only the traditional studies of the public schools in Wales but also the curricula from the sixth, seventh and eighth grades of progressive US schools. As she absorbed the materials, she remembered how more self-confident she became. The intensity of her studies crowded thoughts of her Uncle Arturo and Guillermo right out of her head. Her daily companion Margarita as part of her Uncle Arturo's ill deeds faded from her consciousness.

She felt the pressure of Miss Jones who drilled her every day on mathematics, including elementary algebra and geometry, history, geography and social studies. Two hours a day she wrestled with English, Spanish and French grammar and literature—and other hours in applying the three languages in conversation and composition.

And in the last year, at the eighth-grade level, Leona was introduced to the sciences—biology, botany, chemistry and physics. Her father even installed a small laboratory in a nearby room.

She absorbed her lessons like a sponge. She found herself well ahead of her cousin Maria Elena and the curriculum at the premier parochial school in the country.

The weekly routine included five full days of studies, interrupted on Friday mornings for a one hour visit by Father Gallegos for religious training in preparation for her first communion. On Saturday mornings, she joined her cousin Maria Elena for swimming lessons, no longer at the Country Club but at the home of one of Granmama's inner circle. Saturday lunch and afternoons were spent with her father, at his home or on a picnic. Sometimes, Uncle Felipe and her cousins Luis and Maria Elena joined them.

Sunday she sometimes went to church in the morning with Margarita, the family was Catholic but not overly religious. The main event each Sunday, since the return of Uncle Felipe, was the family lunch in the mansion's dining room, usually presided over by Granmama—with Uncle Felipe, his wife and her cousins sharing the table. Grandfather only attended on special family celebrations of as birthdays, wedding or anniversaries. Leona's father was never present whenever Granmama attended.

For Leona, the special time each week remained Thursday afternoon tea at 4:30. Miss Jones ended classes at 3:30 PM and cleaned up the room in anticipation of the arrival of Granmama. Leona put on a party dress. The great lady arrived just before 4:00. Then began an hour and a half of conversation in French, with Granmama. Miss Jones and Leona discussing the events of their week and occasionally other events of interest to the family at home. Those hours with Granmama she treasured and having Granmama all to herself made her feel special—she so thirsted for maternal affection.

The only real breaks in the classroom routine were the two ten-day visits each year to the finca. They usually coincided with Granmama's periodic retreats to Antigua—those absences lasted a month or so. As Granmama would say at tea, "It is lovely to be at home with my own family." When Granmama was away, Uncle Felipe would be in charge of the mansion—and he often invited Leona's father and grandfather to join them at Sunday lunch.

The trips to the finca Leona considered to be vacations from the classroom. Miss Jones never held classes at the finca, but there was always something to learn. Leona enjoyed the sense of doing something practical—of working in the soil and feeling that she was helping something take form and grow.

And, she had come to know almost all the families on the finca. She liked them and they seemed to welcome her being with them. Her experience with their reaction to bringing up her late uncles Arturo and Guillermo made her more sensitive to their feelings—even though she always remembered Granmama's counsel about "them" and "us." She never mentioned her uncles Guillermo and Arturo again.

Suddenly she focused on the visit to the finca after her tenth birthday. She saw Miss Jones, Margarita and herself arriving at the great house. The foreman Pedro Martinez was striding across the driveway to the car.

He was smiling, "Welcome ladies."

Miss Jones smiled her greeting and said, "Mr. Borakas asked me to deliver this letter to you on our arrival." She handed him a large envelop.

Pedro took it and accompanied the ladies into the house. When he opened the envelop, he found a one-page letter and a manual of about 20 pages. He read the letter and was quite excited. "This is a very important day for me. Mr. Borakas advises me that has promoting me to superintendent of the finca and my three assistants to foremen."

The ladies congratulated him. The housekeeper ran over and gave him an abrazo. She said, "This is the first time in my memory that one of our finca family members has been made superintendent of the finca—it was always a Suarez Moncada family member who lived in this house."

Pedro took a deep breath before continuing, "He has also entrusted me to start a new project tomorrow that he has been planning for some time. He instructed me to carry out the project without his coming up to oversee my work. He has sent me a manual with instructions to replace aging caoba (mahogany) trees with new varieties of shade trees from Colombia and Costa Rica. He says that the new trees that arrived yesterday will give more shade and protection to the shrubs and that these new trees are very effective in increasing the production of berries on the plants—even with less water and fertilizer."

"I want to start the work tomorrow morning. Would you ladies join me in initiating the process? I would be very pleased if you would."

Miss Jones looked at Leona and Margarita, whose smiles said that they would. Miss Jones nodded her agreement.

"I will be here at 7:00 A. M. Is there anything else I can do for you this afternoon?"

Miss Jones said, "No thank you, but I'm so pleased about your promotion."

Pedro replied, "I know the housekeeper has everything ready for you and you will be well taken care of".

As he was leaving, Leona asked, "How are your son Carlos and the other young men getting along at school in Sonsonate?"

She was genuinely delighted when the new superintendent reported, "Carlos and two other boys earned honors in academic studies as well as vocational skills. The Fathers have awarded Carlos a scholarship to complete high school without them and asked me to consider sending him to the United States for university." He beamed as he reported, "The principal Father told me, 'Carlos has the aptitude for engineering and if you are willing, I can arrange for a scholarship for him to study at the University of California in Davis'. Carlos is home now while we decide on his future."

Leona had never forgotten the strange sensation she felt when she sat near him at church that distant Sunday ago.

He kept popping up in her thoughts and she had no idea why out of all the finca children she had met, he had stood out. There was something about how he looked and acted that set him aside from the other finca children, and she barely knew him. But she felt him someone very special.

In her mind's eye, she saw herself at one of the Christmas celebrations. She was seated on the dais smiling hellos to her friends among the finca families when she sighted Carlos alongside his mother. He looked so familiar and so vibrant that she felt that strange sensation again—almost like an electric shock. She seemed confused and looked away before he made eye contact with her.

After grandfather and Granmama distributed the last gift and led the way out of the great hall, Leona lagged behind and went over to greet Pedro, his wife Josefina and their children—but specially to see

Carlos. Leona extended her hand in friendship to the foreman and his wife and wished them a Merry Christmas and in turn their three children, including Carlos. It was then that Pedro informed her that Carlos has been given a scholarship to study with the Fathers in Sonsonate. She noticed that he was handsome with his mother's smile, but his features reminded of her someone else. They had no more than politely said hello to each other when Miss Jones came for her to join the family in the upstairs parlor. And, upstairs in the parlor, her mind was still focused on Carlos.

After the new superintendent left, Leona went to her room to unpack, and she was still thinking about those strange sensations Carlos provoked. When she finished unpacking, with telling Miss Jones or Margarita, she strolled over to the Pedro's house on the pretense of saying hello to Carlos's mother. She knocked on the door, and Carlos answered.

Quite awkwardly she blurted out, "Oh, I am so pleased to see you. Your father told me the great news and let me congratulate you. I just arrived from San Salvador and wanted to tell your mother that I will be here for the next ten days. I plan to go to the new plantings with your father in the morning and I hope you will be coming too."

Carlos replied, "Please come in. I'll call my mother."

Leona stared at the departing Carlos. When his mother Josefina appeared, she motioned for her guest to sit down, she was used to having Leona call on her during the visits and they chatted about Leona's studies and the trip down and life on the finca since her last visit.

Then, Carlos returned to the room with a tray of coffee cups. As he passed the cups around, Leona asked, "How long do you plan to be at the finca?" He replied,

"For the next few months while we decide what is best for our family. My English is not very good and there are several courses required by the university that they don't provide in Sonsonate. And there are all the money and personal decisions that need to be considered."

Carlos turned his head and Leona saw her Uncle Felipe features engraved on his eyes while the rest of his face imaged his mother. Leona found herself confused—no that can't be—I'm seeing things-- and lost track of the conversation. Then she heard Carlos asking her, "Are you fluent in English? How difficult is it to become proficient?"

Leona stumbled as she groped to refocus on the conversation. Then she opined, "Yes, Miss Jones teaches me more in English than French or Spanish. I found English difficult at first, especially the pronunciation. So different from Spanish and French. Miss Jones can give you a better guess than I about how much time it takes to be proficient. I guess it depends on the person and wanting to learn."

Leona found herself saying, "I better go now. I hope you can join me tomorrow while your father starts the new plantings."

Carlos shrugged his shoulders and Leona said goodbye to his mother.

The following morning Carlos accompanied his father when he picked up the ladies for the walk to the new plantings. The superintendent reported, much to Leona's delight, "Carlos will join us each day during your visit. He hasn't had much experience with new planting practices, and it will be good for him to see them for himself."

"That would be fine," said Leona in a matter-of-fact voice while inwardly she was excited.

They walked almost a mile to the plot in which the new shade trees were to be planted. Pedro had overseen the removal of the aged caobas and the land had been cleared and prepared for the planting of the new trees. There were also scores of new coffee bushes waiting to be placed under the new trees.

Then Pedro almost lamenting said, "Ladies, the manual Mr. Borakas sent me is in English. Carlos and I know very little English. We tried to understand what the steps are to plant, fertilize and water these new trees. I need your help in carrying out the instructions. Mr. Borakas warned me that planting and taking care of these new trees are different from what we are used to—and for us to increase the productivity per plant we must do the job just right. With your help, telling us what the manual says, we'll try to get started. I hope that, with your help, I can show the foremen what they need to do to teach to finca workers."

Pedro, with Carlos' help, began to read the manual, word by word. After struggling through the first paragraph, he asked Miss Jones for help. Miss Jones volunteered, "Let Leona, Margarita and I translate the manual for you. Let me see it." Pedro handed it to her.

She read it quickly and said, "I don't think that an oral translation will work. There are technical terms that we require precise translation. We need to write down the instructions for you in Spanish and that will take a couple of days at least."

Pedro looked disheartened. He had very little practice with working from instructions in English. He thought for a minute and then, "I guess that is what we need to do. Thank you for your help." Turning to Carlos, "Go tell the foremen that we have a delay and that they tend to their normal duties today. I will tell them tomorrow when we will start planting the new trees and coffee plants."

Miss Jones asked, "I could use some technical help in the making sure I understand the technical terms used in the manual. I don't want our confusing or misleading you. I know that you are very busy, but do you think Carlos's training with the Fathers in Sonsonate is sufficient to help us as we work through the manual?"

Pedro said, "Yes, the Father taught him well. So, Carlos, you work with Miss Jones. If you get stuck, call me."

So, the ladies with the manual returned to the big house. Carlos alerted the foremen and arrived a short time later.

Miss Jones immediately sat the team down at the dining room table. She translated and Leona and Margarita wrote down her words as the Spanish text. Every so often, Carlos would say. "Excuse me but that doesn't make sense." Then, she would detail word by word until it became understandable. It took several hours to translate the first few pages.

When Pedro came by at the end of the day, it was clear that it would not be until the fourth day that a useful version in Spanish would be ready. So, the plans for the visit were changed. Carlos and the three ladies worked long hours in the dining room of the great house while Pedro and the foremen would work on other projects.

In the late afternoon of the third day, just before Pedro arrived, Miss Jones turned to Carlos and said, "Without your technical and practical guidance, I could not have done this job. You seem to know some English. Did you have any English classes in Sonsonate?"

"No, Miss Jones. None of the Fathers spoke English."

"How did you learn as much as you seemed to know?"

"Oh, Miss Jones, I only know a few words from a book that I found in town. I tried to teach myself."

"Well, Carlos, I will send you a grammar and certain elementary books to help you, to help yourself. Starting right here tomorrow, we will take an hour each day of our visit to work together on your English. You have a real aptitude."

When Pedro arrived, Miss Jones and Carlos went over the Spanish instructions with him—and made sure that the instructions made sense to the man who had to carry them out and plant the new shade trees properly.

It took three long days to complete the translation.

Day four, the ladies were up at dawn and accompanied Pedro and Carlos to the planting site. Father and son, with help from Leona and Margarita, did the work while Miss Jones made sure that each step in Spanish followed the letter of the English instructions.

The foremen joined them in the late morning and Pedro instructed them on the new processes. Carlos and the ladies were the audience unless Pedro called for their help. When noon came, only a few new trees had been planted, but the process of change was underway.

On the way back to the big house, Leona remarked, "That was very interesting. Did you notice how quickly Carlos picked up the changes? He is smart. No wonder the Fathers think him a good university candidate."

The following day the ladies were taken to another area of the finca where Pedro and Carlos introduced them to another new project that did not involve coffee production but improving the food supply for the finca families.

Pedro reported, "Mr. Borakas asked me about the productivity of the finca workers. I told him that performance had been improving since the new water fountain had been installed, the community orchard laid out and the repairs made on some of the adobe houses, but it was still not good. The work seems to get sloppy later in the day. I also noticed that it seems to drop off later in the week. Part of the problem may be their drinking, but I think they don't have as much food to eat later in the week. I told him that I believed the men would work better if we raised the daily food ration of two fistfuls of beans and two tortillas three times a day per family member. That plus the output each family gets from its small subsistence plot and a few chickens, is not enough food to carry them through the week. I also added that I thought the 75 cents daily wage did not cover family needs for items at the town store."

"Mr. Borakas just nodded. But, before he left for San Salvador a couple of days later, he said that diet had a lot to do with productivity and asked for some suggestions for improving the food supply for the finca families. I thought a bit before making a proposal to increase the daily food ration and maybe provide a weekly ration of meat. As Mr. Borakas was turning to leave, I added 'raising the daily wage to one colon would be good."

"A few weeks later, Mr. Borakas authorized me to tell the farm families that we would let them take time off on Friday each week to work on the crops they were growing around their houses and if they wanted to fix up their house, the foremen and I would help them with materials they might need. Mr. Borakas sent me some money to buy tiles for flooring, panes of glass for windows and materials to repair adobe walls and roofs. He also authorized me to give surplus wood for families to build furniture for their houses. We started that work since your last visit. Carlos and I will take you to see some of the improvements the families have made during the next few days."

Margarita asked," How have the families reacted? My grandmother told me that she and my uncles were skeptical about the patron's motives. They weren't sure that once they improved the house, the patron wouldn't take them over for operations and force the families to move."

"I hear of those rumors and try to reassure them. I know the families don't trust the patron, but only time will show that we mean to help them live better."

Miss Jones added, "You are so right Pedro. I remember how skeptical my people in Wales were of the landlords and their promises. Generations of exploitation cannot be corrected overnight."

Pedro said, "The foremen and I are doing what we can, but the families do not always trust even us who have grown up among them. But we are trying."

Then, he changed the subject, "I want to take you now to see the barn for cows and pigs and the new chicken coop that Mr. Borakas sent me money to build. I chose a hectare near the adobes that wasn't needed for operations. I worked with the finca families on a plan for their tending the stock and a system for protecting the animals and sharing all the meat, milk, eggs, and chicken. I hear that some of the men believe that the patron is going to eliminate their daily food handouts and force them to live on what they can produce and an occasional ration from the weekly ration from the barn and coop. I have tried to tell them otherwise, but they are uneasy. I wish

Mr. Borakas had talked to the finca families before he instructed me to build the barn and coop."

"I've put Manolo, one of my foreman who is especially liked by the finca families, in charge of the barn and coop. I'm not sure how this will work out, especially when some of the men get drunk, but we will give it try."

The ladies inspected the new barn and chicken coop. There were a few milk cows, hens and roosters and several hogs. A new supplement to the food supply—but no additional money for the daily wage.

The following day, Pedro showed the ladies several new installations that Mr. Borakas had authorized to make berry drying more efficient and improve the packing processes. Carlos did not accompany them since he was working with the foremen in training the finca workers on the new planting techniques. When he left the ladies, Pedro checked on the progress of the new plantings and made sure that the work met manual specifications—and only a few had to be done over.

After work each day, Carlos visited Miss Jones for an hour of English. She was impressed by his eagerness to learn English. He tried very hard to read and speak, but his progress was slow.   He had trouble hearing the sounds of words so different from how the letters are pronounced in Spanish.

Leona stayed very close by and seemed to hang on his every word and gesture. Leona was feeling something special when she was around Carlos. One afternoon during the English class, she found herself wanting to touch him, to feel him close to her.   She began inching her hands close to his where he was writing out a phrase. She pulled back because she heard Granmama saying something about "us" and "them." She was confused.

As she had so often in her young life, she shared those feelings with Margarita--the person she felt most at ease. What were those strange sensations she had for Carlos—a boy. She had had little contact with boys other than her cousins at Sunday dinners. And they seemed so silly or they tended to just ignore her. She had seen her cousin Luis every so often. He was a couple of years older, but even when he was nice to her, she wasn't that impressed. His sister Maria Elena, her closest friend after Margarita, would tell her how handsome her other girlfriends thought Luis to be, but to Leona, he was just her older cousin whom she did not really care for. But, Carlos, about six years her senior, he was different.

Margarita at first seemed uncertain about what she should tell Leona, she listened to her and thought carefully before responding: "Those are the feelings that Miss Jones talked about when you asked about feelings between a girl and a boy. When you meet a boy whom you find attractive, you get those emotions. Sometimes they seem to overwhelm you, but you must control them until you are ready to get married. Leona, you have many years before you will be ready to be married. So, just admire Carlos and treat him as a special friend."

Leona just sighed. She did not know how to react. She did not understand Margarita's words any more than Miss Jones'. She had lived so sheltered a life that she was not prepared to hear about relationships. And Margarita, the cook's daughter, had taken a big risk in saying that much to Leona. But Leona respected her friend, kept her confidence and realized that she had to control them.

What Leona only leaned later in life

from Miss Jones is that, that evening, after she went up to bed, Margarita approached Miss Jones. "Leona told me that she was having feelings for Carlos."

"Yes, I noticed," was her reply.

"Miss Jones, that is not good. Oh, not because he is the superintendent's son, but, because his blood father is Uncle Felipe. He is her first cousin as much as Luis and Marie Elena."

Miss Jones gasped.

"My mother told me that, when Felipe was a young teenage, he and Josefina, Carlos's mother, fell madly in love. They went to the village priest who married them. When Granmama found out, she was furious. Grandfather had the marriage stricken from the records. But Carlos's mother was already pregnant and, to avoid another Guillermo and Arturo incident, arranged with Pedro's parents for him to marry her. Fortunately, the two liked each other and have built a loving marriage. Pedro accepted Carlos as his own son. My mother believes that they have never told Carlos that his blood father is Felipe. So, you see how delicate the situation is. Leona must not be encouraged to see Carlos, her first cousin."

"Felipe was a favorite of my mother and he shared with her his sorrow. I think my mother has always loved him like a brother but didn't know how to help him. In her situation as the cook, she couldn't say a word when his parents fiercely argued about what had happened, with Granmama blaming her husband's lust for servant girls infecting her son. Felipe was not allowed to come back to the finca even for Christmas and Easter. Grandfather and Granmama arranged to send him to university in Spain hoping he would forget about Josefina. My mother tells me that he has never stopped loving her. My mother remembers that, on his first trip to the finca after his return from Spain, the first question he asked her was about that girl and her child."

"Shortly after his return, my mother learned from Granmama's maid that Granmama arranged Felipe's marriage to the daughter of one of her close family friends in Guatemala—someone Felipe hardly knew. My mother says Felipe never talked to her about his marriage but noted that, whenever she saw them together, they never seemed to be happy. My mother believes that Felipe and his wife never melded, but that he truly loves his two children—and pines for Josefina, the woman he can never have."

"So, you see Leona must not become especially fond of Carlos—except as a cousin or friend."

Miss Jones seemed at a loss for words. After a lengthy pause, "Thank you Margarita. I must inform Mr. Borakas and let him advise me what we should do."

The next day Leona remembered that Miss Jones had kept her very busy at the great house working on advanced algebra equations all day. When Carlos came by for his English lesson, Margarita had Leona on visits to Margarita's grandmother. Except for Sunday at church, in the last few days of that finca visit, she saw very little of Carlos, much less was close to him.

It was only on the next to last day at the finca that Carlos again joined the three ladies and his father. Pedro was introducing him and the ladies to a new plan for moving the dried coffee beans down to the Salvadoran Railway for shipment to the Pacific port of Acajutla or to the International Railroad of Central America (IRCA) for shipment across Guatemala to Puerto Barrios on the Caribbean. Once again, he called on Miss Jones for help in understanding some of the IRCA

Regulations that were only available in English.

Still half-asleep Leona was returning to the confines of her bedroom. She still had warm feelings for Carlos as she looked at the clock. It was just midnight. She felt as if she hadn't been in bed for much more than three hours. She felt just as tired and upset as she had three hours earlier. She realized that she had never lost those feelings for Carlos—feelings that she had only shared with Margarita. Then she remembered that she had once told her father that she admired Carlos, but never that she had deeper feelings. She was almost twenty years old when she learned from her father about Margarita's conversation with Miss Jones, that Carlos's biological father was Uncle Felipe and that he was her first cousin.

And then she thought, "The only one who was interested in my thoughts about the fincas and their people was my father. Although he never went there with me, he was the only one who encouraged me to share my thoughts about the life and work at the finca. She knew now that Miss Jones had told him about her feelings for Carlos, but he kept my secret. He really cared for me."

Leona chided herself for not appreciating how her father had cared for her--not grandfather nor Granmama nor anyone else of the Suarez Moncada inner circle. It was her father who shaped her life.

CHAPTER 13

Leona was now wide awake. She was beginning to read the subliminal messages from her Granmama and to understand how they induced her silence at the meeting. Her disciplined mind told her to continue her inner voyage of discovery until she could put all the pieces together. She recognized that the face in the mirror was her mind scorning her inaction.

She laid back on her pillow and transported herself back to nearly thirty— just weeks after her return from the finca and the manual incident. That was when her childhood cocoon burst.

It was June and World War II in Europe ended. It was Saturday noon. Leona's father had just arrived at the mansion. Miss Jones accompanied her into the library and greeted her father, "Good morning Mr. Borakas. Leona has been looking forward to lunch at your home today. But, before you leave, I want to tell both of you that I have decided to return home to Wales by the end of the year. The War is over, and I ache to see my parents and loved ones."

Turning to Leona, she quietly sighed, "My dear, I have taught you all that I know. I have taken you through nearly eight years of English and US school curricula. I have shared my love of literature and introduced you to my favorite books in English and French. Now, you need to go to a preparatory school that can further hone your fine mind. You, Margarita and I have lived these years almost in isolation, and you need to know the world and the people outside this classroom, this mansion and your fincas. You must learn how to associate with the good and evil that fills the world."

"You know that I am very fond of you and that you will always be in thoughts, but as important as it is for you to learn the world, it is for me to return to my beloved Wales and renew my life with my family and friends there. This will not be easy for either one of us but it must happen. Better now than later!"

"Miss Jones turned to Mr. Borakas, "I know you understand my motivation. I have suggested many times since the tide of War turned that I was eager to return to my home and pursue an academic career. I am truly grateful for the opportunity you gave me, and even more pleased that I had the opportunity to open the world of knowledge to Leona. The experience here has been extraordinary, and you have been most kind to me. But it is time to move on."

Mr. Borakas replied, "Of course, we understand. I will work with you to make sure that the transition is as easy as possible for both Leona and you."

Leona ran over and hugged Miss Jones, with

tears running down her face.

The following Thursday at tea with Granmama, Leona greeted her with the news, "Granmama, Miss Jones is going home to Wales at the end of the year to be with her family. My father says that we will help her."

Miss Jones added, "I believe that my work here is done and that Leona needs to continue her education in a formal school setting, with other children her age and a variety of teachers more expert in the various subjects she must study. I am so grateful to you, Mr. Borakas and your family for this opportunity."

Granmama was effusive in her admiration for Miss Jones and told her, "Miss Jones, you have been a wonderful, dedicated teacher. You have opened the world to Leona and given her the basics for a good life. Your training of her in French is remarkable. You have made possible these special interludes each week when we can find enjoyment through the language of Voltaire. And, yes, your preparation has made it possible for Leona to aspire to attend the same college at Neuchatel where her mother and I had such wonderful teenage years with the dear nuns."

"With your news", Granmama continued smiling at Leona, "I will close up the mansion and take you to join your mother in Neuchatel."

Leona beamed inside. That means that Granmama wants to be close to me. She is proud of me and wants to show me off to the nuns. I will have Granmama all to myself and we can share our lives together.

The following Saturday on meeting her father in the library, Leona burst out, "when Miss Jones leaves, Granmama will take me to Neuchatel to be with her and study at her school. Isn't that wondeful!"

Mr. Borakas was much more pensive, musing, "When Miss Jones departs, I am not sure exactly what will happen. I will talk to Granmama. We must agree on what is best for your schooling."

Leona was crestfallen. Her vision of having Granmama all to herself in Neuchatel was what she wanted.

Her father continued, "I was hoping that you would come to live with me for a few months, while we arrange for you to attend one of the college preparatory schools in the United States. The nuns in Neuchatel maintain a prestigious finishing school designed to prepare noble ladies for marriage and social responsibilities. I am not sure that's the education you need to live in our changing world."

"You are very bright and you should complete your preparation to live in the world of business because in a few years you are to take over the Suarez Moncada holdings. You will need knowledge of world politics and the skills for directing a successful enterprise in that world. And you need to meet and interact with people, men and women, in a more open setting than a nun's school."

Leona was very displeased because she wanted to be with Granmama and the nuns. She almost started to cry when she felt a hand on her shoulder. She looked up and found Miss Jones smiling at her. Miss Jones softly said to her, "Your father's plan is better than going to Neuchatel. In the United States you will become acquainted with the world in which you will have to live. And, if you need me, I will always be waiting to help."

Her father then hugged her and asked that Granmama join them. When she entered the room, she seemed to know what was about to happen. She glared at Leona's father and Miss Jones. Miss Jones took Leona's hand, and they left the library to the shrill sound of Granmama's voice. Leona could hear the noise, but not words of the bitter discussion in the Library between Granmama and her father. In her heart of hearts, she wanted Granmama to convince her father to let her go to Neuchatel.

Granmama did not appear at tea the following Thursday, and Margarita told her that she spent most of the week with her family lawyers and had summoned grandfather over for a long discussion in the library.

The following Saturday, her father picked her up at noon in the library as usual. But that Saturday he was accompanied by Uncle Felipe, Maria Elena and Luis. No sign of Granmama. They left the mansion in her father's limousine and headed directly to his house for lunch.

After they were seated in the dining

room, Uncle Felipe told us, "There are great changes coming to our family in the next few months and Uncle Nicolas and I decided that it was best that we told you together."

It was the first time that Leona had ever heard any member of the Suarez Moncada family call her father other than Mr. Borakas. Leona looked quizzically at Maria Elena, who just shrugged her shoulders.

"You are the next generation of Suarez Moncada family—all three of you. Uncle Nicolas and I hope that you will be good friends throughout your lifetime. I want to tell you now how the Borakas family saved the Suarez Moncada family from ruin and why we need to be united."

"In the Great Depression of the 1930's, grandfather and Granmama had spent the family wealth on trips to Europe and great parties. Grandfathers had borrowed millions of dollars from the

Borakas family bank, and he could not raise enough money to repay. He had squeezed every penny he could from the coffee fincas, including those in Granmama's dowry. Not all of it was legal."

"Well, grandfather went to Uncle Nicholas's father and made a deal. He offered his daughter, my sister Maria Concepcion, in marriage to Uncle Nicolas if the bank would cover his debts and save the family name. After a lengthy negotiation, grandfather agreed to turn over title to all the Suarez Moncada fincas, restore those in Granmama's dowry to her, the marriage of Maria Concepcion to Nicolas and the transfer of title to the Suarez Moncada fincas to the first-born heir of the marriage. That is the reality with which we live.

"I wanted to tell you this myself because the three of you are reaching the age when you will hear gossip and untruths."

Leona burst out, "Am I the child of the agreement?"

"Yes, Leona you are. But, let me continue. Ever since the agreement, the Borakas bank has run the fincas, with Uncle Nicolas as the person immediately responsible. He has invested to increase their productivity and rebuilt them into some of the most profitable in Central America. He has also revived our family fortune and provided us with the means to live comfortably—we are meaning Granmama, grandfather, my sister Maria Concepcion, and you and me."

"For the past several years, he has allowed grandfather and me to take an active role in managing the coffee business. He has consulted with grandfather and me about running the fincas and selling the crops. He has shared with us equitably in the proceeds and indeed made sure that all could live well, that the fincas are modernized and that the families on the fincas enjoy a better life. Those are facts I can attest to, not idle rumors that others may spread."

"We have now reached a time when the three of you are growing up and may well be called upon to participate with grandfather, Uncle Nicolas and me in family discussions—and we want you to accept that responsibility and do everything to avoid conflicts among the three of you."

"Nicolas, do you want to add anything? Children, do you have any questions?"

Luis was visibly upset as he listened to his father and then blurted out, "I am the oldest and the only man in this generation of the family and it is I who should take charge of the family business when the time comes. My mother tells me that is what happens in all the other families."

"Sorry son that was decided by grandfather over a decade ago when the Borakas family saved our family from financial ruin."

Luis glared fiercely at his father—and then at Leona. Leona noticed that look but had almost disregarded it. The ten-year old had never such a look before.

Maria Elena half sobbed to her father, "Why aren't you living at home with us? Why are you living at the mansion?"

Uncle Felipe looked sadly at his daughter and reluctantly responded, "I had hoped that you would not ask that question. The truth is that your mother and I are no longer in love. I thought it best that I move back to the mansion. No, I do not have other lady friends. I respect and admire your mother and will do nothing to hurt her, but we can no longer live together. I do love both of you and want you in my life."

Leona watched him look at his children and again saw a contrast in the teary reaction of Maria Elena and the scornful sneer on Luis's face.

Then Leona's father stepped in. "Other developments in the past two weeks are about to bring further changes to your lives. Miss Jones will be returning to her native Wales in December and Granmama has decided to sell the mansion. She is planning to live in Neuchatel where my wife lives and separate legally from grandfather. You know that they have lived apart now for many years. She is putting her personal affairs in order and will move to her home in Antigua until the mansion is sold. Leona will come to live with me, and Uncle Felipe has arranged to build a house on the lot adjoining this house. He and I will run Sanchez Moncada fincas. Grandfather is retiring and Granmama has had her dowry returned. They both now have separate investments on which to live comfortably."

His matter-of-fact pronouncement did not invite additional questions.

There wasn't much talk through the rest of the lunch. But, as they were finishing dessert, Uncle Felipe smiled at the three children and said, "I look forward to the five of us working together for many years and having you assist Uncle Nicolas and me in running the fincas."

Luis scowled and slumped in his chair. Leona remembered then how unpleasant his face as she tried to reach out to him. Why hadn't she remembered that look at the meeting yesterday afternoon.

Chapter 14

For the next several months, life in the mansion was quiet. Only once did Granmama preside over a large family gathering at which grandfather was invited. She announced that the mansion would be sold, that she would be moving to Neuchatel and that for the next several weeks she would be with her family in Antigua. After lunch, she held court, greeting each of her guests and inviting them to visit her in Neuchatel. She embraced many, but Leona now remembered that she only patted her on her head. The following day Margarita later told her that Granmama was taking her personal maid and the housekeeper with her.

Uncle Felipe became the master of the mansion in its final months. He hosted Sunday lunches to which both grandfather and Leona's father and Miss Jones were invited, along with his wife and children. Sometimes he invited other cousins and non-family friends to liven up the usually quiet, almost subdued table. At the Sunday lunches. Leona heard most of the family news—the progress on selling the mansion, the building of Uncle Felipe's new home adjacent to her father's house, Granmama's schedule for leaving for Neuchatel and grandfather's plans. Business was never discussed nor the frictions gnawing at the heart of her cousin Luis.

The constant in Leona's life remained in the school room. Miss Jones feasted her on literature, science, and history—in French, Spanish and English—subject matter that most students discover in high school. Leona was sole object of Miss Jones's attention. That Margarita was also present was a happy circumstance for Margarita, but it was Leona who was always asked the object of Miss Jones' questions and the one required to prepare essays and other classroom papers. The only other regular visitor to the classroom was Maria Elena, who seemed befogged by her cousin's studies—two or three years ahead of her course work at the premier local parochial school.

During those six months, Leona seldom left the mansion. The routine remained much the same, but no Thursday tea with Granmama and no visits to the finca. It was only on Saturdays that she left the mansion to swim with Maria Elena at a private pool, lunch with her Father and get a glimpse of the world outside.

Yes, the outings with her father! She realized how important he made her feel. He always appeared right at noon, and he never tired of being with her. She remembered that she frequently tried to shut him out—because Granmama always looked annoyed at her Greek merchant son-in-law. Then she also remembered how caring he had been and how he treated her more as a grown-up than a child. She remembered that it was her father who nurtured her affection for the finca and the finca families. It was he who brought her the latest news, sometimes about a new cultivation practice that upped output or some improvement in living conditions.

Yes, she recalled, it was her father who told her that Carlos Martinez had departed for the United States to study English and take required courses at the Christian Brothers School in order to enroll in 1947 at the University of California Agricultural College at Davis—and a question never crossed the ten-year old's mind about who was paying for that to happen. Her father simply said, "Arrangements were made with our coffee broker in San Francisco, and the Christian Brothers report that he has adjusted well and is doing fine with his schoolwork." Leona was excited at the news and wondered what Carlos was experiencing—and almost wishing to be there with him.

Then came that morning in early December when Uncle Felipe convened all the family at the mansion for lunch. He sat next to grandfather at the head of the table. The uncles, aunts and cousins of the Suarez Moncada clan gathered for a pronouncement. Leona also remembered her deep disappointment that Granmama was not there.

At the beginning of lunch, grandfather as head of the family rose and solemnly announced, "This week the mansion was sold to a neighboring government to become its embassy in El Salvador. The embassy will take over the mansion in early 1946 and we have graciously been given a month to six weeks to remove our family treasures. We have loved our home, but it is now time to move on. Felipe and I plan to take a few memorabilia and personal items and invite each of you to identify those which you would like. We will try our best to accommodate your wishes." Grandfather then toasted the family. Leona remembered her deep sense of loss at that moment was not leaving the mansion, but the absence of Granmama.

The remainder of that lunch was animated conversation about specific items that one or another relative had always treasured and longed to possess. Leona noticed that the more the discussion lasted, the more heated it became. She also noticed that grandfather seemed to be ignoring the bantering while Uncle Felipe tried to mediate. When the lunch ended, each family member embraced the other members of the family and then paid their respects quite formally at the door to grandfather and Uncle Felipe.

When the family had left,

grandfather, Uncle Felipe and Leona were left. Grandfather looked wistfully around and said, "I never thought that this day would come. But to return Granmama's dowry, it became inevitable. I have taken the few things that I want. I leave it to you to arrange to divide up the heirlooms and dispose of what is left." The two men embraced. Grandfather patted me on the head, picked up his hat and walked out the front door. Uncle Felipe put his arm on Leona's shoulder, squeezed her lovingly and walked her up to her room on the second floor. Thus began the physical move from the mansion.

By mid-month, Miss Jones closed the school room and tearfully embraced Leona before leaving for the airport for her flight back to Wales. That night, with Margarita's help, Leona packed up her treasures for her new life in her father's house.

Leona had not thought about that

lunch for many years—she had buried it. Now as she sat up in bed, wide awake, she realized how it shook up that sheltered existence of the classroom with Miss Jones. She remembered how frightened she was of what her new life would be like without Miss Jones and above all, Granmama. She didn't want her life to change. Then she recalled how bitter she felt toward both her Uncle Felipe and her father, especially her father whom she barely knew—one Saturday afternoon a week! Why hadn't he thought to ask her what she wanted? But, then, what could she expect because he, as Granmama so often had told her, was only the son of a Greek merchant, not an equal of a Sanchez Moncada. And she also remembered that young Leona had ached in those final days at the mansion to be packing to go with Granmama to Neuchatel.

CHAPTER 15

Leona found herself at sea in those last days in the mansion. Everything that made up her world was changing. Miss Jones departed. Granmama was in Antigua. The classroom was packed up to move to her father's house. Some of the service staff went with Granmama. Others, like Margarita's mother, were planning to move to Uncle Felipe's new home. A few had found new jobs in the city or were returning to the countryside to live with family. The order and routine that protected her was gone. And she blamed her father, the Greek merchant, for it.

she remembered that day shortly before Christmas 1945 when Margarita helped her pack a small suitcase to leave the mansion for the last time. She looked around her bedroom and classroom for the last time—feeling very frightened and alone. Margarita took her by the hand and led her down the stairway past the library to the front door where her father's Cadillac was waiting to take her into a new world.

That day she was heading back to the finca for the annual celebration of Christmas. She sat between her father and grandfather in the back seat. Margarita was in the front seat next to father's chauffeur. This year Granmama would not attend—she had cut her relations with the Suarez Moncada clan and rejoined her family in Guatemala. It made Leona sad just to think about not having Granmama with her at Christmas—and then there would be all those dreary future years when Granmama would be in Neuchatel, not having weekly tea with her. Leona felt too alone to even cry. It was a desolate trip to the finca even though her father held her hand and made sure she lacked for nothing.

At the finca that year, grandfather was the lord of the manor. He was given center stage. Uncle Felipe, his wife, her cousins Maria Elena and Luis, were the only other family members who joined them. Grandfather for the first time she could remember gave her much more attention and affection than he did to her cousins. The four-day visit turned out to be much happier than she expected on leaving the mansion.

There were festive lunches and dinners every day. Even her cousin Luis seemed to be enjoying being there. Leona, Margarita and Maria Elena played and talked together—and took long walks around the finca, primarily because Leona wanted to say hello to the finca families and see how the recent improvements had worked out.

That Christmas ceremony was very different from prior years. This year the family chairs were not on the dais at the head of the room, but on the floor level as were the finca families. While the format of the ceremony was cast in the mold of prior years, each family receiving a gift and each child a toy, the greeting by grandfather was much more personal and caring. In prior years, once the farm families greeted the patron and received their gifts, they departed to spend Christmas with their families in their adobes. This year a festive table was set for the finca families to share Christmas with the patron and his family.

When the formal greeting ended, grandfather, Uncle Felipe and her father invited the families to join them in a toast to Christmas at the large table at the other end of the room that, during the ceremony had been filled with Christmas goodies and a punch. The families seemed uncertain how to react, but everything changed when grandfather walked among them, greeting many by their first names — something she had never seen while Granmama defined the protocol. Felipe and her father personally led families to the table. Then, Leona and Maria Elena, hand in hand, encouraged others to share the bounty on the table. It was so unlike previous Christmases.

When Leona saw Josefina, Carlos's mother, she embraced her and asked, "What have you heard from Carlos? I understand he is in California studying with the Christian Brothers. How does he like being in the United States? Is he doing well in his studies?"

"Carlos writes us once a week and tries to make us feel that he is in the room with us. He loves the experience in that country. He tells us that it is so different from El Salvador—where there aren't the great differences between people, you know, your family and we finca families. He says that the mathematics and science classes are more challenging and complex than those he had with the Fathers in

Sonsonate. English has been difficult to learn, especially the pronunciation—words are often spelt differently than the letters would lead you to expect. He tells us that it has been very hard, but he is now making acceptable grades—hopefully good enough to be accepted at the University at Davis."

Leona noticed that her Uncle Felipe edged closer to listen in on the conversation and she saw the eyes of Carlos' mother focused on those of Uncle Felipe—and that mere glance told her that there was a special affection between them—she didn't understand what that was but she had seldom seen that kind of look between two people.

Leona replied, "I am so happy for Carlos, He is a wonderful person."

As she said those words, her father came over and asked her to join Carlos's father Pedro and him. With a smile Leona joined her father. The two men were talking about the improvements to which she had been introduced during her last visit to the finca.

Her father nodded to the Superintendent, "Please repeat what you just told me."

Pedro began, "The situation on the finca is very uneasy. The barn and chicken coop were misunderstood. Many of the families thought they were steps by the patron to reduce their daily food quotas. Others believed that the patron was getting ready to reduce their daily cash wage. Very few have taken advantage of the supplies to improve their house—they think that there are strings attached. I have tried to explain that the improvements were intended to improve their diet and housing without any cost to them."

"Then a week ago Saturday after the men went to the cantina and spent most of their monthly pay on aguardiente, they returned to the finca with their machete drawn. They burned the barn and the chicken coop, killed the hogs and absconded with the chickens and cows. I tried to calm them down, but they accused me of selling out to the patron. Margarita's grandmother, who is the most respected grandmother among the finca families, calmed them down and got them to disband."

"We have done little work since that night. The foremen and I have been working alone—and I fear that, until I leave, the finca cannot get back to normal."

Leona's mouth dropped open. She remembered the story of her Uncles Alberto and Guillermo.

Her father said, "Pedro it is best for you to take your family to San Salvador. I will arrange a new job for you with the farm machinery company. Without your expertise the tractors and other equipment would have stopped working long ago, and that company is looking for a trouble shooter who can service their equipment across the country."

After a brief pause, he asked, "Which of the foreman is the best to take over—not only technically but also for calming down the situation on the finca."

Leona almost stopped listening as the two men continued. She just stood frozen with trepidation until her father took her hand and walked around the room to wish the families assembled a Merry Christmas and Prosperous New Year.

Then they left the reception. Her father took to the small office he had set up off the main family room of the great house. He sensed her confusion. He tried to explain what had just happened.

"My dear, I wanted you to hear why Pedro and his family are leaving the finca.

Not because I want them to go, but because some envious finca families think he sold them out to the patron. We are the patrons, me, Uncle Felipe and grandfather. Unfortunately, centuries of ill will between the native people and those like us who conquered them and took over their land and lives have built a wall of distrust. It will take lifetimes to destroy that wall. Even with the best of intentions, when we as a patron try to help, we can never forget their distrust. I decided what to do without talking to them and letting them tell me what they thought they needed. They must believe that I, the patron, was not about to trick them with false gifts."

"Your and my task is to preserve the family inheritance, but to do that in this new world of instant communications we must take the time to build understanding with those whose help we need to preserve that inheritance. I have been trying to that since I took over managing the finca from your grandfather and Granmama. I have tried to give opportunity to the sons of the finca families through education and managing the finca. I didn't realize that I was also building envy and discord among the finca families."

"But, daddy, I can't understand why they would turn against Pedro. He knows so much about coffee planting and seems so good at getting jobs done—and he always treated the workers and their families so nicely."

"I have no doubt that Pedro is the most talented manager among all the finca men and has grown in the job. Most respect him, but many believe that he is no longer one of them. They all know about his wife's love affair with Uncle Felipe. They all know that grandfather arranged for him to marry a pregnant woman. They know that grandfather also gave him a better adobe than his father's and promoted him to more responsible jobs. Then I sent him to Sonsonate to the farm management course and made him foreman when he returned—and then superintendent—and then arranged for his son with Uncle Felipe's blood to not only school in Sonsonate but university in the United States. I never took the time to talk to the farm families about my respect for Pedro's competence and my plan to have all the key jobs at the finca filled by the most capable finca people—from among all of them—and that I was prepared to educate them and their children if that be necessary. I also did not take the time to talk with them about improving their living conditions and health—that I need them and their help to raise productivity on the finca and increase their share of the profits from increased productivity."

"Oh, dear, I don't think that you understand what I am saying now, but I want to educate you so that you will understand."

"It is my fault that Pedro and his family must leave, but I have a good job for him in San Salvador. To calm down the finca, I will name the foreman that the people trust most to replace Pedro and let him select his team. That will be the signal to the finca families that there is no further need for violence."

Leona came back from being a ten-year old to the mature businesswoman she had become. She sat up wide-wake in bed and said out loud to whoever could hear her, "I'm ashamed of myself. My father had tried to tell me what to do. Why hadn't I focused on her father's words that Christmas night, instead of being lulled to sleep by Luis's mouthing of some phrases from Granmama."

CHAPTER 16

Almost without thinking, she found herself back at the Christmas visit to the finca and the ride back, not to the mansion but to her father's home. She was riding in the car again with her father, grandfather, and Margarita. She saw herself driving up to and then through the opened steel reinforced gate at the entrance to the large house that her father had built in the San Benito suburb. She had been there before many times for lunch, but now this was to replace her haven in the mansion.

She heard her father saying to his chauffeur, "Take Mr. Suarez Moncada to his home and then return here."

He then took her hand as Margarita opened the door and led her up the few steps to the front door of the spacious French Provincial house. With Margarita at his heels, he led Leona past the butler to the large circular stairway to the second floor. Leona mechanically walked up those stairs again and saw for the first time the open area at the top of the stairway that gave way to a hall on both side of which were three doors to the bedroom suites. She remembered how she had then wished that the hand touching hers had been that of Granmama or Miss Jones, even as her father said, "Dear Leona, this is your home now."

He led her down the hall to the last door on the right and opened the door to an elegant sitting room that as she looked in she saw all her prized possessions from the classroom at the mansion and a second room beyond that seemed to be a replica of her bedroom at the mansion-- her father had made it look as close to her corner of the mansion as he could.

She remembered her smiling father leading her to the picture window in the sitting room and saying as he pointed down,

"With the new swimming pool, you, maria Elena and Margarita can swim any time you wish. That is my Christmas present to you this year."

Leona remembered how the dread of leaving the mansion gave way to a good feeling that the place she had always felt safe had been transferred to her new home. She looked up at her father and smiled a "Thank you." She remembered that her father hugged her and went on leaving her to get settled, he turned to Margarita, "Your room is across the hall and you will be much closer to Leona than you were in the mansion."

She heard the glee in Margarita's voice as she opened the door to her elegant bedroom suite—and she watched as Margarita hugged her father—she saw in Margarita's eyes a ray of happiness that she had never seen there before.

This was to be Leona's—and

Margarita's home for the next thirty years. The Borakas family built it as the home for their son Nicolas and his bride Maria Concepcion. The bride never chose to live in it—she stayed at the mansion until her child Leona was born and then left for Paris. Nicolas lived in it alone for almost 11 years—until he brought the two girls to live with him.

The house occupied almost a full city block, inside an eight-foot-high wall, whose top was studded to jagged pieces of broken glass. The entrance, with a sentry box, was the large steel gate embedded in the front wall. Adjoining the wall in front of the house was a three-car garage, with a second story three room apartment where the chauffeur and his family lived. Near the center of the two-story French Provincial style home, situated to catch the breezes that freshened San Salvador almost every afternoon of the year.

The house itself was elegant. Nothing seemed crowded—and it had large spacious rooms and hallways. Its cement frame was filled with wide windows to catch the breezes and light up the interior.

On the first floor, to the left of the entrance hall next came the formal living room. Next came the formal dining room whose French doors on the right side opened into the large family rooms that overlooked the back patio and terrace. The kitchen area was set behind the dining and family rooms. To the right of the front door was the library, a bar and the master suite that only Leona's father had occupied in his lifetime. The second story was meant for the children of the marriage—Leona turned out to be only one.

Leona remembered her own ambivalence then—her missing the mansion, Miss Jones and Granmama but, returning to the present, sitting on the bed in the same suite that she first entered before her eleventh birthday, she felt a sense of shame for not recognizing the love of her father and how he had tried to make her life in his house as much like her old refuge as possible.

And the years living in the house had been happy ones. She remembered the joy of Margarita with her suite across the hall and the pleasures they shared together it was the second time that evening that she focused on her special relationship with Margarita. This time almost like a revelation. Leona had always taken for granted that Margarita would be there for her—never had she focused on the person Margarita—a woman with a life that she needs of her own.

Once again she chided herself. "Do you realize that in those thirty years you never asked her what she wanted to do or how she felt. You never asked if she had preferences or even if she had a boyfriend. It has always been about you helping me. I always treated you as a 'them.' You never refused me anything—but I never bothered to find out how you felt. I have always done what I thought was right—I never thought of talking it over with you." She suddenly shook, all over.

CHAPTER 17

Life in her father's house revolved about Leona.

The first days in the house Leona and Margarita settled in, arranged things in their respective suites to suit themselves. They enjoyed the pool almost every afternoon. Dinners were with Leona's father and Uncle Felipe. Uncle Felipe was settling into his house next door, with Margarita's mother as his housekeeper.

Two weeks after they had settled in, her father called the two girls to the library for a family talk. He started out, "Are you two young ladies comfortable and enjoying your new life." Bothe enthusiastically replied, "Yes."

"Well," he continued, "it is time to set a routine that includes formal schooling. I don't plan to hire a new tutor. Both of you need to meet more young ladies your own ages and to complete your education. Leona, my dear, I think you are too young to go away to school in the United States. I truly want you with me here for at least another year. Margarita most of your schooling has been with Leona and Miss Jones, and you will need at least a high school diploma to assure your own future."

"So, I have looked around at the schooling available here and find that the parochial school which Maria Elena attends is the best now available here. It offers most of the courses required for admission to US, European and Latin American universities and it is accredited to most. I plan to take both of you tomorrow to the school to meet with the administrator and have you duly enrolled. I will take you to school every morning and arrange to have my car pick you up each afternoon."

Margarita looked very surprised and humbly sighed, "Thank you very much. I will try to do my best and be worthy of your trust." And, turning to Leona, she continued, "We can learn together to deal with the outside world." Leona just looked at bit overwhelmed. Somewhere deep inside of her, she wanted to be with Granmama in Neuchatel, not in San Salvador with her father, the "Greek merchant." She did not look forward to attending that new school.

The following day, the Sister administrator was happy to meet with Mr. Borakas and the two girls, but thoroughly confused about which grades they should be assigned.

"Good morning Mr. Borokas," she began. "I have reviewed the reports of Miss Jones and the certificates she prepared on both young ladies. Leona is not quite 11 and Margarita is 16. It appears that they both completed all of the course work for the first eight grades, except religion. Their scores are indeed impressive, but I will need to have them pass our own tests to see in which grades they should be placed."

"For her age, Margarita should be placed in the fifth year of high school a year from graduation. Leona at 11 in the second, where her own contemporaries are grouped. I will give them the examinations for their respective years. If they pass, I will enroll them accordingly."

Mr. Borakas noded, "that seems to be appropriate."

The administrator continued, "I have arranged for them to take three tests this morning: Spanish grammar, mathematics, and history. About 40 minutes per test. Tomorrow, I will have three more ready: Spanish literature, basic science, French and religion."

Turning to Leona and Margarita, she asked, "Do you think that it would be too much to take three tests this morning or would you like me to space them out."

Leona replied, "Miss Jones often gave us two examinations one after each other in a morning or afternoon. I think that we can try. If we get too tired, we can ask you to space them out. What concerns me more is that we haven't had time to prepare for the examinations."

The Sister administrator agreed, "First, we will see how tired you are after each examination and decide then whether to continue today or spread them out. Leona, for our purposes we want to evaluate your base of knowledge and we don't assign materials before we have prospective students take these tests."

Mr, Borakas remained in the office while the administrator led the two young ladies down the hall to a classroom where the tests were laid out. Both young ladies set to work.

Both young ladies finished the test on Spanish grammar well before the time assigned. They saw no reason not to tackle the second. Again, they finished well before the time assigned and agreed to take the history test. For each of the examination, Miss Jones had already covered the subject matter.

In the car returning home, Margarita said, "The mathematics examination dealt with elementary algebra. Miss Jones has already introduced us to trigonometry," Leona observed "My math questions didn't even reach the level of elementary algebra. It was like my talking to Maria Elena about what Miss Jones was teaching us and her not understanding. The tests were very easy."

The tests the next day were just as quickly completed. Even without any classroom courses on Catholicism, they had ready answers to almost all questions from

Father Gallegos had taught them in his weekly sessions over the past four years.

Leona recalled that the following Monday, the Sister administrator called Mr. Borakas and informed him, "Both young ladies scored very high grades on all the examinations and Mother Superior and her staff would like to meet with both the young ladies before assigning them to classes. Mother would like to meet with you and them tomorrow morning at 10:00 A.M. if you are available."

The following morning at 10:00 A. M., they entered the Mother Superior's conference room where Mother and four teachers were assembled. After introductions, Mother said, "We are pleased that you young ladies are about to enter our school. We were surprised by the maturity and accuracy of your tests and thought that we should talk with you before making your grade assignments."

Then began a two-hour conversation about the subject matters to be covered during the forthcoming academic year. Mother and the four teachers asked the two young ladies a variety of questions, sometimes in French and Spanish, on literature, algebraic equations, French grammar, European and Latin American history and geography.

At noon, Mother thanked Mr. Borakas and the girls, saying, "This has been an unusual experience for us because of the high-test scores. The four nuns are the lead teachers for high school grades three, four, five and six. We wanted to meet the young ladies and then decide where best they should be placed. We normally do not like placing a young lady in a class above their age contemporaries, but the test scores indicated that their base of knowledge acceded that of their contemporaries in our school. So, before we decided, we wanted to meet with the young ladies themselves."

Mr. Borakas said graciously, "Thank you for your consideration." The girls also nodded their appreciation.

Mother smiled and said, "We will talk together and advise you of our decision by next Monday. Oh, lest I forget, all of us thank you for your most generous contribution to the school. It will allow us to upgrade our science laboratories this year."

On Monday, Mr. Borakas was advised that Margarita would be placed in the senior class and Leona in the third year— both with age groups older than they would normally be assigned.

Thus began a scholastic routine that lasted throughout 1946, with a recess at Easter, a six-week vacation from July through the early August celebrations of Christ the Savior of the World (Salvador del Mundo in Spanish), and graduation in December. The maid woke up the two young ladies at 6:30 AM every morning—

time for showers and some juice. The chauffeur drove them to the school in time for morning prayers and breakfast, three hours of classes to noon and three hours of classes to almost 4:00 P.M. Almost every afternoon they took a dip in the pool homework and dinner with Father or Uncle Felipe presiding. Leona frequently wondered what the routine at Neuchatel would have been like—and how wonderful it would be have been like to have Granmama joining her after school for tea.

The school year 1946 rolled by. Neither girl was challenged by the subject matter. Both had to learn to lie with other girls, some of whom were not always friendly. It took Leona some time to adjust to a routine in which she was not the center of the instructor's attention and the resentment of her classmates to her answering all the teachers' questions. Her cousin Maria Elena, one grade behind her, cued her in to being less eager to display her knowledge.

Margarita had a different problem. Every one of the girls knew that her mother was the family cook and deliberately snubbed her. This was nothing new for Margarita because most of the Suárez Moncada family had treated her with disdain. Margarita warm personality and resolute calmness won over several of her classmates to befriend her. Margarita just ignored the others.

Neither made friends easily. They had lived their lives in the mansion and little interaction with outsiders. Leona now realized that her Father sensed that and invited their classmates to parties at the pool. He always bought nice presents for them to give to classmates at birthday parties to which they were invited. He treated Margarita with the same tender hand that he showed Leona. Leona always enjoyed herself, but never stopped wondering about what it would have been like in Neuchatel and with Granmama.

Both girls scored at the top of their respective classes. Most of the subject matter they had already studied in more depth under Miss Jones's tutelage, and Miss Jones had taught them how to study and how to analyze the assignments given them. They had to be ready every day on every subject for Miss Jones. At the school in classes of 25 they might be called on once or twice a week in each course—and they were always prepared.

The most important event almost every day at father's house was dinner. They dressed up and ate in the large dining room, with her father presiding. If he was away on business, Uncle Felipe did the honors. Dinner was time for conversation and exchanging ideas on the events of the day. Father always asked Leona and Margarita about their progress at school, and he would tell them about his day and the local and international news. Father always asked questions and encouraged both the girls to do the same.

Many weekend evenings, father would invite diplomats, civic leaders, business associates and university professors - with their families—to join them at the table and discuss local issues of interest, new books or the changes in the world order that World War II wrought. Some weekends, Uncle Felipe often brought Maria Elena and Luis to swim in the afternoon and stay on for a family dinner. Despite the efforts of Uncle Felipe and Maria Elena, Luis never treated Leona nicely—he seemed always to be telling her that he, not she, should be in line to run family affairs when their fathers passed on.

A business associate who was invited several times that year for a weekend dinner was the former superintendent of the family fincas, Pedro Martinez and his family. Mr. Borakas clearly respected Pedro's competence and arranged for his hire as an equipment technician at the local farm machinery company and from the stories discussed at the dining room table, his bosses and their clients applauded his work. While Mr. Borakas never mentioned it, Margarita's mother learned that it was Leona's father who helped Pedro find and finance a fine house in the Flor Blanca neighborhood where the family had settled in comfortably.

When they came to dinner in early June, Pedro and Josefina brought good news of Carlos's earning high grades at the Christian Brothers High School and his rapid improvement in English. They also announced, "Carlos will be coming to spend the month of July with us. He has received a commendation for his studies and an A in English." He smiled at Mr. Borakas—guess who had bought the ticket?

Leona the eleven-year-old, blurted out, "Oh, that's great news. He can join us every Saturday at the pool and we can have a month-long party." In fact, since she would be on school vacation for all month, she wanted to have him all for herself. Her feelings for him were unlike anything she had felt for any other boy—even though Margarita kept reminding her that he was her blood cousin. He was the only man that Leona could remember dreaming about.

As it turned out, in spite of all her hoping and planning, the July day that Carlos arrived on the Pan American flight from California, Leona and Margarita were at the family finca with her father and Uncle Felipe to meet with the lead foreman who had replaced Pedro and discuss with him both production issues and social relations. Carlos was met by his parents and siblings— and they introduced him to their new life and surroundings.

This visit to the finca was particularly important to Leona's father last Christmas that led to Pedro's departure. Grandfather, Uncle Felipe, Leona, Margarita and her cousins Luis and maria Elena had presided over the Easter ceremonial visit, but Leona's father had been in Europe on a business trip. While there had been no news of difficulties at the finca, Leona's father was uneasy not knowing personally how the new lead foreman was working out and the reaction of the finca families to his leadership. Was the new lead foreman up to the job? Had the finca families accepted one of their own as the new boss? Her father felt that, given her affection for Pedro and his family, she had to learn for herself that business takes precedence over personal feelings.

It was late June, just two days before Carlos was due home, that father decided on a three-day visit that ended up lasting a week. When they arrived, they were greeted by the housekeeper who seemed surprised by the visit. She apologized, "Patron I did not expect this visit. I must fix up the house for you—and arrange to get more food. The bedrooms are ready and most things are in order, but there are many other tasks to be done to ensure that you are comfortable during your stay."

Leona's father said, "Don't worry. I just decided to come up for a few days. We can make do with what you have on hand."

"Oh, thank you patron," she replied.

"Would you please send word to Mr. Yepes, the foreman, that I would like to talk with him tomorrow at 7:30. We plan to be here for only a few days and want to spend them with him."

The next morning promptly at 7:30 Mr. Yepes, Manolo to all the finca, walked into the dining room. He was about 5'5' tall, stocky build, and his dark skin and flat broad face portrayed that he was Pipil ancestry, not much diluted by Spanish blood. He matter-o-factly said, "Good morning patron."

Mr. Borakas replied, "Good morning Mr. Yepez. Please come and sit down with us at the table. I think you already know Mr. Suarez Moncada, Felipe, my daughter Leona and Margarita."

As if taken by surprise, he moved to table and nodded to the each of those already seated.

The housekeeper brought in a platter of fruit and a pitcher of coffee. There was already a basket of fried plantains, a bowl of beans and tortillas on the table. Mr. Borakas then said, "Please help yourselves. We can have breakfast as we talk."

Mr. Borakas invited the housekeep to join them. She took a seat next to Mr. Yepes and began passing the food around the table. Mr. Yepes was completely taken by surprise—he had not expected to be invited to eat at the table or to have the housekeeper eat with them.

After a few minutes, Mr. Borakas began, "Mr. Yepes, you have been the main foreman here since Christmas. It was Pedro Martinez who recommended you, and all the information I have received tells me that you are doing a good job. The production figures are high and there are no reports of any troubles."

Mr. Yepes looked straight ahead, not directly at Mr. Borakas as he replied, "My name is Manual, but everyone knows me as Manolo. I would be pleased if the patron also calls me Manolo."

Mr. Borkas replied, "My name is Nicolas—not patron. He is grandfather, next is Felipe, Margarita, and Leona. Those are our names, and we'll call you Manolo and you call us by our names—not patron. You are our foreman at the finca and we must work together."

There were nods of agreement before Mr. Borakas said, "We have come to work with you the next few days and to get to know you better. We want to discuss your views on running the finca. And, I want my daughter, who will succeed me as the owner of the finca, and our good friend Margarita to share the experience."

Manolo showed no emotion as he responded, "I am ready to work you as long as you are here. I have worked with Miss Leona and Miss Margarita on their many visits to the finca. I worked with them on many different operations under the direction of Pedro. You know he is my good friend. How is he and his family liking the city?"

"Very much," chimed in Leona. "They have a nice house and Carlos is coming home this week on vacation from the

United States."

Manolo nodded his head and replied, "That's good news. All of us will be pleased. Pedro has been my brother and teacher since we studied together with the Fathers in Sonsonate. He understood the technical part much better than I and he always took time to explain to me what I didn't understand. He used to say to me, 'Manolo, you know how to get the people to do the job—you and I go together."

They leisurely ate the breakfast and then Mr. Borakas asked Manolo to schedule the next few days, Leona noticed how her father let Manolo take the lead in their inspection of each of the operations. She also noticed how the finca families respected Manolo and listened to whatever he told them. Pedro was more like a teacher than Manolo—which she admired—but the finca families had not reacted personally or trusted him as they did Manolo.

The second night when Mr. Borakas, grandfather, Uncle Felipe and the two girls sat at the dinner table after eating, Mr. Borakas asked the two girls what they had noticed during the inspections. Margaritas said thoughtfully, "The operations seem to be going very well. In some ways better than when Pedro was in charge. I think Manolo is the difference. He not only knows what needs to be done, but the workers trust him. There is something in the way he treats them that is different. Pedro and Manolo both come from finca families, but Pedro would do what he thought needed to be done. My grandmother told me, 'Pedro never talked to us. He just did it.' I noticed yesterday and today that Manolo takes the time to talk to the workers and finds out what they think and what their problems may be—and then helps them get the job done."

Leona nodded her agreement as did grandfather and Uncle Felipe. Father then noted, "All of us agree with you Margarita. Manolo is the boss now. He asks, listens, and then responds. He acts differently than Pedro. They are very different people. Pedro somehow is more like us, the patrons. For centuries, we have made all the decisions that affect their lives—always thinking of our own interests. We made decisions for them. We were Lord and Lady Bountiful to whom they came to ask favors in times of trouble—and our responses were their last resort."

He continued, "So, when Pedro and I wanted to improve their lot, we just did the things we thought they needed. We changed their morning routines. They got upset. They didn't know what our intentions were. I guess they thought that we were going to cut back on their food ration or monthly wage to pay for the barn and coop. Who knows what they feared the changes would cost them—seldom had changes in the past benefited them. I wonder whether they feared we were preparing to cut the daily food ration or even their small monthly cash wage."

"Tomorrow, I want us to consider asking Manolo about calling a meeting of the finca families to ask them what we can do to help them improve not only operations on the finca but also the way they live. I think the mistake that Pedro and I made last year is that we never consulted the people about what they wanted and needed."

Leona was startled by the idea—so contrary to the "us" and "them" of Granmama's catechism but, as she sat at the table in the finca that night, the eleven-year old thought, "It does make sense to ask people about what they want before you do it for them." Granmama had shaped her interpretation of what her father was proposing.

She had not remembered that dinner for many years and as she thought of that night, she now understood how Granmama's conceptions had warped her thinking and how much she missed her father's point. He was not proposing more of we helping them, but of we and they working together to improve our understanding each other and making changes beneficial to us both.

Leona remembered that at breakfast the following morning, they discussed the possible meeting. Grandfather could not remember that there had ever been such a meeting in his lifetime.

The housekeeper pointed out, "I have been tending this table for over thirty years and do not recall anyone even raising such an idea." Turning to grandfather, she continued, "When I was a little girl, I remember your father spent a lot of time with the finca men and they respected him as a good patron. I remember stories of his sitting down and talking with the farm families as you are proposing. I simply don't know how the families will react."

When Manolo arrived, it was Uncle Felipe who asked him what he thought about the their meeting with the finca families. Manolo said, "I don't know, I have never thought about it." He just sat for several minutes, letting the idea mill round in his mind. Then, he looked at the Suarez Moncada men and opined, "I like the idea if you give a day or two to sound out the families. They must understand the purpose of the meeting and what you want to discuss with them. Can you stay until Sunday? Because Sunday would be a good day for the meeting. Would you want the meeting here at the great house or would you consider having it somewhere else? The finca families are not usually comfortable when they come to the great house."

Mr. Borakas responded quickly, "Yes, we can stay through Sunday and you choose where we should meet."

As Manolo was turning to leave, Mr. Borakas asked, "We have time to look at the repair facilities and discuss plans for replacing some of the older bushes and installing some additional cover trees. Just tell me when you are available."

"I'll be back in an hour," Manolo nodded. "I am concerned about the facilities in town for housing the seasonal workers at picking time. We need to organize better our hiring procedures and reduce the disruptions for the finca families that the onslaught of those laborers on our finca life. We will need a substantial number of pickers this year because as I showed you, the shrubs have so many more flowers than in former years. Yes, sir, we have a lot to talk about."

The next few days were full—

inspections discussions and planning, with the Suarez Moncada men letting Manolo take the lead. Each afternoon, Margarita visited with her grandmother, and Margarita reported that Manolo had talked individually to each family, explained the purpose of the meeting and urged all to attend. Her grandmother said that Manolo said the families could listen to Mr. Borakas and then they could tell what they think and worry about. "We have never had such a chance before."

Manolo suggested to Mr. Borakas, The meeting should be held out-of-doors. I think the open area near the adobes and the well would be a good place. We can use those benches in the great hall and invite the finca families to bring chairs from their houses. I can move a few chairs from the great house for you to use."

Mr. Borakas agreed, "Don't bring the chairs used at Christmas and Easter—just simple, straight-backed ones that are in the superintendent's houses."

"Agreed." Said Manolo.

"You open the meeting Manolo and introduce me."

Sunday afternoon sometime after 2:00 P.M. the meeting began. Almost every man, woman, and child of the finca families were there. Manolo began, "I am the foreman and your friend. I've asked you to meet with Mr. Borakas and Señor Suarez Moncada because they want us to work together to improve not only the production of coffee but our life on the finca. I've talked and worked with them for the past week and they have asked my opinion, not given me orders. So, let me ask Mr. Borakas himself to talk directly to all of us."

Rising from his chair, Mr. Borakas began, "Good afternoon to each of you.

Thank you for coming. You have lived and worked on the finca for many years—through the bad times and the good ones. You know how to grow coffee and I want us to work together to grow better quality and more coffee beans. We have spent the week with Manolo to do just that—and I expect Manolo will be here for many years to manage the finca."

"I also want you to tell Manolo and me what you think can be done to improve not only production but to make your lives better. We want to get your ideas and help you as much as you help us. Manolo and I want to hear how you want the adobes improved and together what we can do to increase the food you have to take care of your children and yourselves. We can't do everything at once—any more for improving your lives than we can to increase production. There are problems which we have to overcome one step at a time. It takes money to buy trees, coffee bushes, fertilizers, irrigation systems. It takes money to improve food rations, raise wages, improve adobes, get milk cows. We need to use the money wisely and plan to do a little more each year to make improvements."

"And I want you to tell Manolo and us what you think needs to be done so that we consider what works and what doesn't work. For the good ideas, we then need to plan how to get them started—what materials we need, how to obtain them and how to pay for them. We need to figure out how to tell each other about plans, problems and progress. That's what I hope we are starting today."

As he sat down, there was an immediate buzz among the people. Manolo stood up and asked, "Would anyone like to say anything?" And several people started shouting at once. Many of the comments were negative. Manolo then shouted to everyone to sit down and put up a hand so that he could let them say their peace. The meeting lasted almost until nightfall. As the afternoon wore on and the people got used to talking to Mr. Borakas, the tone became increasingly friendly.

A lot of talk started that afternoon that has continued for nearly thirty years— until yesterday, with Manolo serving as the bridge between the Borakas-Suarez, Moncada and the finca families. In fact, only two days before the meeting, Leona had been with Manolo at the finca to initiate new projects. Many of which had emanated from suggestions of the finca families.

Reliving that Sunday at the finca as she lay in her bed, Leona heard her father speaking loud and clear: involve the finca families in your decision-making process. In today's world of advanced technology and communications, you can no longer impose your will and play Lord and Lady Bountiful.

She also heard her cousin Luis championing the antithesis in the same language she had heard from Granmama. Why in the world hadn't she recognized the retrogression at the meeting and reacted?

CHAPTER 18

The following day she was on the trip back to her father's house and the visit of Carlos. She saw him at the swimming pool, a muscular Adonis—the man to which she unconsciously had compared every other man in her life. He had treated her with warmth and understanding of a friend— maybe a younger sibling, but never as object of passion or desire. She smiled as she put that in perspective.

Suddenly she saw her cousin Luis was also in the pool, so less impressive than Carlos. She recalled noting how Luis resented Carlos's presence and did everything he could to disrupt Carlos's efforts to teach his younger siblings to swim. It took a warning from Leona's father to make him back off. She saw an evil look in Luis's eyes that she didn't understand at the time.

She had seen the same threat in his

eyes many times over the years—especially when her father or she gave him an order or forced him to change one of his schemes. Luis's eyes were the harbingers of his inner feelings. She had considered him a bitter ineffective nobody—until yesterday's meeting. She sat up in bed as she realized that she was the object of his bitterness. It was dawning on her that he thought that he, not Leona, should be head of the family and its fincas. He was furious that she respected Carlos, whom his mother had repeatedly referred to as "his father's bastard." He shared his Granmama's and mother's distain for Mr. Borakas.

She shook her head at her bad judgment and swore an oath to herself. Very deliberately, "I still have control of family assets and Luis will get not one cent of them."

Chapter 19

Leona was now assessing what she should do next. Her thoughts immediately focused on Tio Umberto, Colonel Umberto Underraga, who had been her father's friend and adviser for as long as she could remember and he was her unofficial godfather.

She recalled that afternoon when she returned from school to find Tio Umberto and her father talking in the library. As she walked into the room, her father said, "Leona my dear I want you to meet my close friend Captain Underraga. He will be having dinner with us tonight."

Leona said, "Pleased to meet you sir."

He smiled and said, "You are even prettier than your pictures. I have followed your growth since you were a baby. Your father always tells me about how smart and charming you are, I want you to call me Tio

Umberto."

Leona excused herself, took a swim with Margarita and dressed for dinner. At the table, they discussed Margarita and her day at school, the state of the coffee market, the emerging rift between the US and the USSR and the weather. Her father and the Captain encouraged the girls to express their views. The dinner was exciting and lasted far longer than usual.

The Captain looked at his watch about 8:00 PM and said, "It is time for me to return to the barracks. I have some matters to clear up. Nicolas, I had a special time. I like your two young ladies and would adopt them if I could."

Throughout the evening the captain called her "Princess" and asked her to call him "Tio Umberto." That did it. He became her *de facto* Godfather—closer to her than most of her blood relatives. She smiled as she remembered how warmly he embraced her when she went up to bed after dinner and how every time they met over the years she always felt that same affection.

That night was followed by many more dinners throughout her year and a half at the parochial high school. He and Leona grew closer together. He told her, "I have not married, I have no family. Your father is like a brother to me. And you are a special young lady in my life. Whenever you need help, always call your Godfather."

She also recalled that over the next several months, while she was enrolled at the parochial high school, Tio Umberto frequently came to dinner. Her father and he talked candidly of their business and political relationships. They trusted her instinctively and she knew instinctively not to mention those discussions.

When she went to the United States for prep school, Yale and Harvard Business School degrees and at her marriage, Tio

Umberto always sent lovely personal gifts but very seldom did he make a trip outside El Salvador. She observed over the years at school or on a trip, whenever a serious problems arose at home, it was Tio Umberto who alerted her father and had a plan to deal with the issue. When her father died suddenly of a heart attack and she assumed direction of the Suarez Moncada coffee operations, Tio Umberto made the arrangements for her to bring back his body and lay him to rest. She knew the two men trusted each other—almost instinctively understood their bond.

It was to her Padrino she would turn as soon as she was ready to act.

CHAPTER 20

As she was putting together the pieces of her life, she was realizing that her father started teaching her when he hired Miss Jones. It was his plan to prepare her for succeeding him as the head of the family business. What else had he taught her to do: survive on her own.

At Christmas 1946, just before her twelfth birthday, Margarita and Leona reported to Leona's father that the nuns were only repeating materials in both grades that Miss Jones had already taught them. They were not very happy with their rote style of instruction after that of Miss Jones. Leona urged her father to send her to Neuchatel. He said that she needed an education to prepare to live and do business in today's world, not learn the fineries of a dying one.

So, her father took her on visits to several all-girls prep schools in the United States. They agreed on one in Connecticut where father liked the curriculum and Leona liked the environment. Father had her enrolled for the spring classes that began in February.

Leona remembered that February. It was cold with snow patches on the front lawn as her father led her through the front door of the academy—a large ivy covered building with classrooms and laboratories on the first floor and living quarters for the select all-girls students on the second and third. Her father and she met the headmistress, and with tears in his eyes, her father hugged her and let her go. An aide to the headmistress led her to the second floor to a bedroom set up for two. She had never shared her bedroom before, and she felt very so alone, far from her home in San Salvador and no Margarita nearby. She remembered thinking, "I wish that I were in

Neuchatel."

Within an hour, her roommate arrived. She was as lost as Leona was. They were both away from home for the first time and seemed to share the same anxieties. And it was Tessa consoling her roommate, Somehow Miss Jones had imbued her with an inner strength or dealing with the new and usual.

She adapted quickly. With her discipline for studying, she became the "brain" of her class, graduating with first place honors. While she was the short swarthy Latin girl in a sea of sophisticated upper class gringas. Leona knew the answers in chemistry, physics, trigonometry, calculus, French literature and all the tough subjects. She was always available to help a classmate. She absorbed all the subject matters and added German and Russian to the languages she spoke.

She also learned to dance, fix her

hair, play tennis and golf and enjoy fine arts. At first, her roommate usually had to fix up dates for her, but then she came to know some boys from the all-boys prep school down the road—and she had a boyfriend or two--learned the right moves at the right time to turn off heavy petting trysts.

Her father took her every year for a month in Europe. He always arranged to accompany her to Neuchatel for a visit with Granmama and her mother. He would drive her to her grandmothers luxurious flat, just a floor above her mother's. She would give her father an embrace and the doorman would take her suitcases and assist her to her grandmother's apartment where Granmama would be waiting—never once was her mother also waiting.

Granmama would give her a gentle hug while the maid, whom she had known at the mansion, would take her bags to the guest bedroom and unpack them for her. Leona always came with presents for her Granmama and mother, usually a piece of jewelry that her father had selected and something Leona had personally picked out in New York before boarding the transatlantic plane.

Granmama planned the week. Her mother came in dinner and often went on excursions to Geneva, Interlocken, Lucerne and Bern. There was always a visit to the siters who ran the college at Neuchatel— with Grandama's constant message about what she was missing and how incomplete her preparation for being a true lady like her mother and grandmother. And there was the ever present "them" and "us." In those four years of prep school visits, Granmama showed Leona most of the important sites in all of the cantons of Switzerland and burned her catechism into her granddaughter.

Then, her father would pick her up at the front door and they would visit the cultural centers of Europe, from London to Istanbul.

The second trip to Europe during those prep school years, her father decided it was time for her become aware of family's lineage, so, he took her to his family's ancestral home in Salonika, Greece. The trip from the Suarez Moncada to the Borakas involved their flying from Geneva to Salonika, the once vibrant multiracial city of Thrace which Miss Jones had introduced to Leona in history lessons. At the great port city, they went to the Borakas family villa reduced to a rubble by the Nazi during their occupation of the city during World War II. It had been the seat of the family for hundreds of years.

Her father lamented, "I came here as a boy to visit my great aunts and uncles— into a magnificent complex of houses and gardens that resembled palaces in Istanbul. When his villa flourished under the Eastern Roman Empire, the Ottomans, and the Kingdom of Greece, it was a center of financial, commercial and civic life—open to everyone in this great trading center—Greek, Moslem, Armenian, Sephardic."

"Our first-known ancestor was a sea captain in the thirteenth century who was licensed by the Emperor in Constantinople to trade with Asia Minor. When the Ottomans came, the family accommodated to the new reality and received new imperial concessions in trade and banking. The family made alliances with the Venetians, the Sephardic Jews exiled from Spain and the Papal envoys from Rome. We intermarried with Catholics, Ottomans and Jews as required to promote and protect family interests—but its core remained true to the Orthodox Church."

"Thus, it thrived for centuries until

the Italians and Germans came. Most of the family moved to Istanbul, and the Germans took over the villa for some purpose or another and leveled it when they departed. You will meet some of your cousins who returned here after the War, but they chose not to rebuilt—leave as another tragic reminder of the family's past and senseless destruction."

Leona looked out at the Thracian Sea and around at the tragic ruins. She was absorbing that her heritage was much broader than Central America and coffee but included multinational finance and trade. Her father was not just a Greek merchant but the member of a great merchant family. Leona was moved by her father's account but still kept hearing Granmama's disdaining words deep in her inner self.

The following Christmas vacation, after the visit to the finca, her father took her to Panama for New Year's to meet his siblings, her aunt and uncle. That branch of the Borakas clan had been established in 1910 when the Panama Canal was about to open. The head of the family sent his youngest son from Salonika to establish a ship chandlering outlet. He married the daughter of a Dutch Caribbean family and sired three children: Leona's father, his older brother, and younger sister. The Panamanian family prospered and diversified into financial management and banking throughout Latin America and the Caribbean. Leona's uncle now ran regional operations and took special care of his younger brother, Leona's father—the two men looked almost like twins. Her aunt married into one of the great families of Panama, a Rabbi whose father helped found independent Panama. She was introduced to the closeness of the Borakas family and the degree to which they looked out for each other.

Her father was carefully exposing Leona to the world that existed well beyond the mansion, with Salvador and coffee production. He was trying to show a world well beyond that of "us" and "them." A world of opportunity and tragedy. A world in which one could prosper if he or she put the right pieces together—and one in which he offered her his strong family support.

And with each experience Leona was shaping her own vision of the life she wanted to live. She was coming to know who she really was. She knew that the traditions of both sides of her family. She knew that she would inherit lands and financial resources when she succeeded her father. But she wanted to do more.

In her studies from day one with Miss Jones and now in prep school, she felt that she had a responsibility to use her wealth for more than her pleasure and comfort. She had real feelings for the finca families, and she wanted to help them—and all like them—to better their life conditions. She was confused about how to do that. Granmama would have her maintain tight control and play Lady Bountiful. Her father seemed to be telling that the old "we" and "they" didn't really work and that the people affected had to play a role in shaping their own destiny. The experience at the finca showed that change required "us" to lead but then Pedro Martinez had to depart because "they" didn't understand why change was taking place. Her courses in history and sociology provided all sorts of variations at different times and circumstances. As a teenager, she wrestled with how best she could do and help those she wanted to help.

CHAPTER 21

Graduation from prep school was a great occasion. Leona was the valedictorian of her class—an almost unanimous choice of faculty and classmates—because not only was she an outstanding student but the one to which her fellows had turned when they needed help. Not only did her father attend but Tio Umberto, Uncle Felipe, Maria Elena and Margarita came up from San Salvador, as did her aunt and uncle from Panama. Granmama flew in from Neuchatel—as Leona learned later life from Uncle Felipe that her father insisted on it.

She earned admission to Yale. The transition was much easier. She was accustomed to roommates, some of whom she really never felt quite at home. She mapped out a course of study that centered around business, economics, sociology and the liberal arts. She was known as the swarthy Latino "brain" who aced her classroom work and helped others with their assignments. But she had matured into a 5'5" svelte, well-figured coed with a social life. She had a love affair or two—and found herself comparing each of her lovers to Carlos, the Adonis of her youth—and none matched up to what she thought being with Carlos would be like.

Even though she apparently breezed through Yale Magna cum Laude, she had dark periods in which she wished to have been in Neuchatel with Granmama nearby. She wondered what her instruction would have been like, how her life would have evolved and if she would have been more satisfied. No matter how much her father did for her, she kept yearning for Granmama—and never really stopped hearing the older lady repeat "he was only a Greek merchant." No matter how much she admired her father or what he taught her, in her inner self she felt like the little girl that sought Granmama's eye and absorbed her catechism of "we" and "they"—and never to forget how "we" must help our country and people better their lives.

Over those eight years she always spent Christmas at home in San Salvador. Every year on Christmas Eve, grandfather, her father, Uncle Felipe and his family, and Margarita drove up to the finca where they greeted Manolo and the finca families.

From afar, she kept in touch with Margarita—letters by the dozens as they shared their separate experiences. Margarita enrolled in the National University and earned her law degree. Leona flew home to share the occasion. At the graduation dinner, her father invited Margarita to join his lawyer's legal firm— and she did.

Leona also kept in touch with her cousin Maria Elena. She took a week off from her freshman year at Yale to attend her cousin's graduated from the nun's high school and joined her when she enrolled at a Catholic college near San Antonio, Texas. She was Maria Elena's maid of honor when she married into a Texas cattle family before she was graduated.

Her cousin Luis went to Salamanca for his higher education, but like his father before him he dropped out without a degree. After a year of drifting, his father, Uncle Felipe, brought him to work in managing the coffee fincas.

Her father brought her occasional news of Carlos. He had transferred to the university of California Berkeley and had graduated in mechanical engineering—in the top third of his class. He had been hired by an international engineering firm headquartered in San Francisco.

In her sophomore year at Yale, grandfather passed away and she flew back for the wake—she met his grieving second family for the first time. The woman he had loved for over twenty-five years was not his legal widow because of Salvadorian Law and Granmama's refusal to agree to a divorce. Grandfather recognized his three children and left his personal assets to their mother.

In her junior year, she returned home to be Margarita's Maid of Honor when she married a fellow lawyer. Leona's father walked her down the aisle and Uncle Felipe hosted the wedding reception. Margarita was no longer living in the suite across the hall from Leona's.

Each summer at Yale, her father continued to take her for a month to Europe, always arranging for that special week with Granmama at Neuchatel. Leona stayed in Granmama's guest room and accompanied her on her rounds of appointments. Occasionally they took a trip outside Neuchâtel, but, whether at the apartment or on the road, every day at 4:00 P. M. they had tea together-- occasionally her mother joined them. Leona hung on every word and gesture from her grandparent.

Some summers her father and she stopped off in Wales at the lovely bungalow her father had given Miss Jones in 1945. But those stopovers became awkward when Miss Jones became Mrs. David, the wife of a widower college professor with a small child. Leona's affection for Miss Jones never wavered and they had become inveterate correspondents.

She found herself smiling at those remembrances of happy times. She filtered through various experiences over those years and focused on a hot July day in Paris when she was walking with her father up the staircase in the Louvre where you get the first sight of Nike, he took her hand and said," The best is yet to come for you. Let's enjoy each moment we have together." It was that spirit that imbued their trips through the mid-1950's to the countries of Western Europe slowly recovering from the ravages of World War II. She smiled as she remembered her visits to the art galleries of Paris, Florence and Amsterdam, her steamer rides down the Rhine, the vistas from the Swiss Alps, the fun and food at the Tivoli in Copenhagen and the beauty of the islands around Stockholm. She thought, "My father had very good taste for just being a Greek merchant."

More important than college vacation was Leona's emerging vision of what she wanted to accomplish in life. She saw herself as more than a Salvadorian businesswoman, but an innovator in the transformation of her country from being just a coffee producer to one with a diversified economy. She wanted to contribute to creating better opportunities for poor people like the finca families to educate themselves and find good paying jobs. She envisioned a country with political liberties like she saw around her in Connecticut, but she wasn't sure how "we" would interact with "them."

In her economic classes, she learned about the movement to form a Central American Common Market and to strengthen the ties among the six countries of the region. As she wrote in one of her term papers. "The Common Market can provide the framework for expanding economic growth, creating jobs and opportunity for attacking the widespread poverty in the member countries and broadening the participation of people in the economic and political life of the region."

At her graduation party in New Haven, she told her father that she was ready to return to San Salvador to not only join him in his business but also help develop her country.

With Miss Jones, she had studied the history and geography of Central America. Most of her readings dealt with the Spanish conquest and colonial history. The few books about the post-independence era were of six republics plagued by a succession of military dictators and agricultural economies dominated by a few powerful land-owning families, including her own. The region was classified as underdeveloped and not noted for its scholarship or fine arts. She could only recall one class on Spanish literature in which a Central America poet was mentioned, the Nicaraguan Ruben Dario, whose brilliance blossomed in Argentina. There were few Central American statesman celebrated in history and economic studies seldom mention the region except to note that it produces coffee and depends on metropolitan North America and Europe for its capital and manufactured goods.

Well Leona wanted to do something to change the character and direction of El Salvador as part of a transformed Central America. She envisioned her future not merely as a vibrant part of her father's business but as a promoter of political, economic, and social change—someone who would help people as she had worked with students at prep school and Yale.

CHAPTER 22

On her graduation from Yale, her father took her to Europe for a month—a whirlwind trip that allowed her three days with Granmama while he did some business in Basle and Zurich. Then they spent a month in the United Kingdom, exploring almost every corner of England, Scotland, and Wales, ending up at Cardiff. It was at Miss Jones' (now Mrs. David) home that he made the announcement that Leona was to be his special assistant in the family business on their return to San Salvador. He was going to teach her personally from the ground up—just as she had been taught the workings of a coffee plantation.

On her return to San Salvador, Margarita and Uncle Felipe met them and had them home in no time. When she opened the door to her suite, she found it refurbished in elegant Louis Quinze style furniture that she has so admired at the

Louvre and an original Picasso and Matisse in her sitting room-office. Once again, she reflected on her father's affection and taste.

For next several months, she went to the office every day with her father. One of her tutors was Margarita, now a member of her father's legal team. Margarita primed her on Salvadoran corporate law and the workings of the legal system. She was pregnant but that did not slow her down. She made sure that Leona learned how to the "I's" were dotted and the "t's" crossed.

Leona quickly found out that over the past eight years her father's scope of operations had grown far beyond running the coffee fincas of the Suarez Moncada family. His success in increasing output and productivity had encouraged other coffee producers in Guatemala and El Salvador to hire his management skills—at a fee. He also benefited from his family banking business in Panama which hired him to turn around production on foreclosed agricultural properties throughout Central America.

So, Mr. Borakas had built up a staff that included Uncle Felipe, Pedro Martinez and three US trained agronomists. Uncle Felipe oversaw the Suarez Moncada fincas and Pedro, the others in country. The three agronomists supervised work at the other Central American fincas and plantations. Margarita told Leona that her father tried to hire Carlos when he graduated with Berkeley, but a major engineering firm in San Francisco beat him to the punch.

Leona, just 21 years old, found learning the business was hard work, but fun. She found a standardized reporting system in place, detailing for each property the costs, inputs, and production. She studied all the reports on the soil, climate, water availability, operating cost, production, and marketing. Then with her father or Pedro or an agronomist, she visited each one, studied the operations and arranged to meet informally with the foreman and workers. She prepared her own evaluation and checklist which always included a section on working and living conditions—with specific suggestions for making improvements. She also included a section on the need for and impact of seasonal laborers required for the harvest with suggestions for improving the hiring and management of managing seasonal workers.

Except for two weeks of rest over Christmas, her first year out-of-Yale was all business.

However, as Leona reflected on the nature of her father's business, she focused less on production and more on marketing. She found that profit margins depended more on market prices than on improved production methods. She began to study regional and world markets for each of the products in her father's stable— variations in prices throughout the year and in different world markets.

For the next two years she tried to concentrate on learning from her father how he marketed company products in the various world markets—his analytical process for evaluating the principal markets, his contacts for selling each of the company's products, and the terms and conditions prevailing in each market. She accompanied her father on every marketing trip he made. She left it to Uncle Felipe, Pedro and the agronomists to deal with production and other problems on the various farm properties.

When she was approaching her 25th birthday, Leona said to her father," I think that we should get out of the production side of this business and concentrate our operations on marketing. We should move our central office to the US. I read of such companies in econ classes at Yale. I think our best immediate investment is for me to go to a first-rate business school with courses on international marketing. I know you know the dean at the Harvard Business School. Can you see if he would consider accepting me?"

Father called the dean. Leona sent him her magma cum laude Yale records. He accepted her for a course that began in the spring of 1960. A year and a half later she not only earned an MBA but developed professional relationships with professors interested in supporting the Central American Common Market and creating a Central American Business School. She found herself meeting with advisers to the newly elected US President, John Kennedy, and to working on papers outlining ways in which the new administration could support the Common Market. She also prepared a detailed business plan to reinvent her father's company.

In the summer of 1960, a series of personal tragedies afflicted her father's business. Uncle Felipe was killed in an automobile accident on the way home from the family finca. He had hired his son Luis to work with him on the oversight of the Suarez Moncada fincas. Luis was very careful not to rock the boat, but, once his father had passed, he subtly took over his father's responsibilities and introduced management changes that resembled practices discarded by Mr. Borakas and his team in the late 1930's.

That same summer, Margarita's husband died of cancer, leaving her with a young daughter and lots of debts. Leona's father helped out with the debts and invited her to move back to her old suite in his house, with her daughter in the adjoining room. Until mid-1962, Margarita was too busy being a mother to go back to work and to see what Luis was doing.

In the fall, Pedro accepted a job in California to manage a large fruit ranch in the San Joaquin Valley that Carlos found for him. Pedro, Josefina and their other two children made the move, leaving no one in the home office to keep an eye on Luis—except Mr. Borakas—and he was out of the country marketing for months at a time. Luis hired his own team and began making his own connections with like-minded coffee producers and military officers.

When Leona returned to El Salvador in the fall of 1961 everything at her father's office looked the same—except the cast of characters. She knew no one except Luis, and she considered him second rate. He had gone to Salamanca, earning mediocre grades before dropping out. After wandering around Europe for a couple of years Uncle Felipe placed him in the company working under his supervision. In their years working out of the same office, Leona paid little attention to Luis's unflattering comments about her and her father—shrugging them off as not important - just her incompetent cousin's perceptions.

Indeed, Leona now realized that she was so absorbed in her new endeavors that she gave little thought to work in San Salvador, much less to Luis. Her immediate goal was to sell her fathers the new business model she had elaborated at Harvard. She proposed opening a new business based at Coral Gables that concentrated on marketing Central American coffee and other food products in the North America and Western Europe. The company would make long term marketing agreements with Central American producers, partner with them in building processing, freezing, canning and other facilities in Central America to increase value-added in country—thereby taking advantage of the Central American Common Market incentives.

At Harvard she had prepared the prospectus for a reformed company, with analysis of risks and financial implication, legal requirements, and market conditions. She had consulted with Harvard professors on her concepts and analysis—and those who were interested in developing a business school for the region had indicated they would consider consulting assignments in setting up the reformed company.

Leona and her father spent several days at Granmama's home in Antigua, carefully considering every aspect of her proposed reformed company. Her father gave the house to Leona on graduation from the business school. He had purchased it from Granmama when she needed more resources in the early 1950's —Granmama was entrenched in Neuchâtel and had no interest in ever visiting her native land again. Mr. Borakas had made repairs and modernized the electrical network, the bathrooms and kitchen. Leona was thrilled—it was comfortable, cozy and private—and it had the feel of Granmama in it.

After several days of intricate discussions, her father and Leona flew to Panama to discuss the business plan with the Borakas banking group. Answering their questions and overcoming their skepticism was no easy job, but she did. Then, armed with their financial and business support, they flew to Coral Gables and set up a new multinational enterprise, of which the Salvadoran office was only a subsidiary.

The next eighteen months were a whirl of activity. Putting the pieces together and getting it running was Leona's primary focus. Her father and the agronomists lined up producers and identified value added projects. With his business record and family resources, Mr. Borakas was a respected businessman and had little trouble signing up new accounts.

Leona's Harvard connections got her invitations to meetings in Washington on the Alliance for Progress, luncheons at the newly established Inter-American Development Bank, seminars at Brookings, planning sessions on US aid for the Common Market and even a small working dinner at the White House with the President and his brother Robert. She was also invited to join an advisory group set up by the Secretariat of the Common Market and Central American Development Bank. Her company was making money and she felt so very important.

Leona remembered those exciting two years with a special glow of satisfaction even though they ended with the cold look at reality that her father forced on her.

During those halcyon years, she noted that her father spent most of his time in San Salvador. It was his base of operations and the Suarez Moncada coffee fincas the base on which he built his business. And Leona remembered being brought back down to earth when he summoned her to a week-long meeting at home in San Salvador—a meeting with only three participants: Leona, her father and Margarita.

Her father warmly welcomed Leona home. He said, "I am so proud of your accomplishments over the past couple of years. Your business plan has started very well, your contracts with the major food companies were more than I anticipated. Now, I think it is time to see where we are and try to anticipate the problems that lie ahead in fulfilling those contracts."

"You know production in Central America is not always reliable and we need to be prepared to do everything necessary to ensure that we meet our quotas. Those big companies aren't easy on suppliers who don't meet the production levels specified in the contracts. We need some quiet time to analyze production levels and bottlenecks."

"Tonight, we'll have a quiet family dinner with Margarita and Blanca. You will be enchanted with Margarita's daughter—she is like a grandchild for me—of course, until I have one of yours to thoroughly pamper and enjoy—something I missed when you were young."

The following morning over coffee, the three assembled in the library. Her father said quietly as he looked at Leona, "You adroitly took advantage of your contacts in the US and the Common Market to build excellent working relations with several major US and Western European food companies and you negotiated very solid contracts to supply Central American products into their networks. We have been signing up a good number of farmers in Guatemala, Honduras, Nicaragua, and Costa Rica to supply the produce due under the contracts. But I want to make sure that they can provide us with a stable flow of products required. We need time to examine realistically where we are now and make sure that we can perform."

Leona was clearly taken aback, "Why are you concerned? I have followed the business plan and sharing your concern, I lined up more producers that the plan calls for."

Her father responded, "That may be fine, but can the farmers meet your deadlines with the quantity and quality products called for by contracts with the food companies? Look, my dear, my concerns come out of years of business experience in Central America, underlined by my efforts to revive production levels at the Suarez Moncada fincas. Meeting production quotas is no easy job, especially when you are relying on others."

"Even when I was in charge, it took me nearly six years to reach profitable production levels on the family's three fincas—and they were among the best run in the Isthmus, but the practices were outmoded, with production dropping from years of little or no investment in new bushes, equipment or worker training. I had Miss Jones take both of you to our main fincas periodically so that you could see for yourselves the time and effort it took to change the traditional ways in which the finca operated and teach new ways of working and living to finca families."

"In the countries of our region, you can't just import new equipment and management practices. You have to build a new work ethic for both management and the workers. You have to open their minds to learning new skills and systems. The patron, who has all the power, can order changes, and force them on an unprepared work force—that usually leads to dispute and often revolt and bloodshed. Or the patron can take steps to minimize the risks that change brings and show the management staff and workers that changes benefit them."

"What I am talking about is what my family has had to deal with in Europe and Panama when it was forced to take over properties after defaults on loans. It took time and training, as well as new equipment, to make the changes profitable and then establish sound operating systems that enabled us to sell them at double or triple what their value had been. That's how we made our money. We found that to the make money in the new economy required more than new equipment and management practices. It required a different work ethic that included a new understanding between "us" as patrons and the managers and "them," the workers in the field."

"Both had to learn new skills to do their jobs more efficiently and that meant a different relationship between the patron and the workforce. And that Borakas family banking experience is what I followed on the Suarez Moncada — fincas and I repeat it took me six years before I could be assured of the quantity and quality required by my purchasers."

"Now, in my family's experience, each workplace turns out to be unique usually because of the people involved and their history. I had to find out what would work on the Suarez Moncada fincas, especially because of the personal relationships that went back generations. I tried to open a dialogue by improving the adobes and providing the water well, but the finca families considered them gifts of the patron who had responsibility to take care of his peons. Then I thought making Pedro, born of a finca family, the superintendent, would turn the trick, but the finca families considered that a payoff for his marrying Josefina and raising Carlos. Only when I made Manolo foreman, whom they deemed to be one of them did they begin to open to us and start talking to us about what they needed to become a working partner with the patron, not merely an obliging peon."

"Well, dear, I want us to review the situation in each of the production units with which you contracted to supply produce. I want to make sure that the conditions on each one reassure us that it can meet the quality and quantity needed. And, if not, what reserve accounts or other financial arrangements we need to make to protect us from non-compliant."

"That experience has made me very

careful. I applied it each time I acquired additional properties—and I have not found any short cuts. The reality is that Central America is only beginning the transition to a twentieth century business model. We are just beginning to shed the old Spanish colonial modes of feudal land ownership and government concessions to operate private enterprises. We don't have the production models and experienced farmers of North America and Europe. Landlords still tell peons what to do—and most landlords are not inclined to invest in the land, much less the work force. And to borrow money to make investments they put up collateral greater than the loan—and most Central American bankers just hold money until the loan is paid off—as Spanish banking tradition demanded."

"Next week I want to look over every agreement the company has entered into and analyze the conditions in each property and make sure that we understand our potential risks. We need to assess what additional assistance our suppliers may need and their estimated cost. Finally, we need to determine what reserves we must set aside in the event production levels by our suppliers fail to meet the targets we expect. I want to be prudent and be able to meet potential problems that could torpedo our long-term viability."

Leona was taken by surprise. She almost resented her father's implication that she hadn't done her due diligence. Then she heard a message from Granmama saying, "We are the leaders who must protect them "them" from "their" inabilities. We" know what is best for "them." She placed that special twist to her father's effort to ensure the company was being diligent.

Leona seemed confused when the first case study was the current situation of the Suarez Moncada fincas. Her father said,

"I lured Margarita back to the office because I was uneasy about Luis. Unlike his father Felipe, Luis never seemed straight-forward and he seemed to be reverting to old ways in running not only the Suarez Moncada fincas but also those under management contracts. I needed someone in the office on a regular basis to understand what was going on. You can never take anything for granted even when you think you have everything under control."

"My concerns mounted when Tio Umberto, who is now in charge of Army Intelligence, warned me to keep an eye on Luis because he was making friends with the most reactionary-elements of the army—those who wanted to return to the old days of the Martinez dictatorship, with military licensing of the private sector participation in the Common Market and stamping out the emerging Social and Christian political movements. The Colonel also told me that he suspected Luis of using our company funds in courting those officers."

"Now that Margarita is back in the office, she is carefully reviewing Luis' reports and consulting the foremen like Manolo to make sure the production records and office accounts are accurate. Since Margarita's return, a nearly two-year dip in production and profits has seemed to melt away. This is an example of why we need a system for monitoring our operations and those with which we have contracts."

Leona bristled, "Well father I have contracted an audit form to check all their books and I think that is enough." Her father shook his head.

"No, my dear that is not enough," he replied and then turned to the analysis of a contract supplier in Guatemala.

That was beginning of the week-long review of each company with which Leona had made contracts and it showed how few really in-depth studies Leona's teams had made of the inner workings of the producers with whom they had made contracts. It was a sobering and trying week for Leona.

The lessons of that week, especially the warning about Luis and his proclivities, awakened Leona to the critical role her father had played in her development as a successful corporate executive. Since his death nearly five years ago she had taken control and followed her own intuition, not always consistence with the prudence her father had enforced.

As she sat up in bed, she felt that she alone was responsible for what happened at Luis' meeting. She had ignored disturbing reports from Tio Umberto and Margarita—she had more important things to do. She sat by because she thought Luis too incompetent to outwit her. She was too busy hobnobbing with experts in the US on eliminating supply bottlenecks and improving her stock's value on the New York Stock Exchange to take care of trivial issues such as her cousin Luis. She had forgotten until it was too late the importance of details that her father had been so careful to watch.

She was in receptions with members of the Kennedy entourage at Harvard and in Georgetown. She was among the mourners when Kennedy was assassinated and in meetings at Cambridge with the professors who had led Harvard's team that created Central America's first business school, INCAE. She was engaged in meetings with the leaders of the Common Market as they discussed their policies and plans. There were those special sessions in San Salvador and Antigua that she hosted for fellow finca owners on private land reform projects.

Those meeting had absorbed her time and interest---little did she tend to the details so important to her father's business model.

Then there was Corey, dear, wonderful Corey. She was attracted to him when they met at a White House conference. A Ph.D Harvard economist, he came to Washington as an adviser to the Kennedy White House. Meeting him was not the electric feelings she had experienced when she had been with Carlos but an intimate glow of respect and enjoyment. Corey and she enjoyed being with each other. He was interested in her work and she in his. They developed a warm, mature relationship. Anyway, she had learned on a trip to San Francisco that Carlos had married and was raising his own family.

In 1966, close to her thirty-first birthday, Leona and Corey married in a quiet civil ceremony in Charlotte, North

Carolina, close to the university in which Corey was teaching. Her father gave her in marriage. Her cousin Maria Elena was her matron of honor and Margarita, her only bridesmaid. Granmama flew over from Neuchatel; her mother did not. Luis and a few other Suarez Moncada and Borakas relatives made up her witnesses. Her husband's family and old Kennedy colleagues outnumbered the bride's friends. Leona remembered her special satisfaction that Granmama had crossed the Atlantic to share in the occasion—her presence was her blessing—everything from Granmama meant so much.

Her marriage also contributed to her losing sight of the details in her business operations. She tried to run her marriage and her business—and she had thought admirably. But, now, she realized that she had subordinated the business details to her new relationship with Corey. She loved being with him, sharing herself with someone else—something she had really never done before. She mused that before Corey, she was the "we" and everyone else, maybe except Granmama, was "they." She was almost ashamed to recognize this reality about herself—but as she looked at herself inside, she had to admit that before Corey she had never really shared anything of herself.

Leona reluctantly admitted to herself for the first time that she had let a lot of business matters slide because of the glamour of national and international politics and her own love life.

CHAPTER 23

Leona's mind now was wiping out the cobwebs of Granmama from her thought patterns and replacing them with the lessons she learned from working with her father. She anguished over how long it had taken for her—a prep school, Yale, Harvard Business School graduate—to realize her own misguided perceptions.

She was near to tears when she thought again of her father and how much he did for her. Whatever she wanted, he seemed to get for her—in spite of the opposition by Granmama. "What have I done to the people who most care for me?" she almost cried out loud.

Three years later, Leona remembered that her father told her that he was worried about the load that she was carrying—public affairs, marriage and CEO of a multinational corporation with tie-ins with a hundred private producers in underdeveloped Central America. He made a trip to San Francisco to try to persuade Carlos to return to San Salvador as chief of corporate operations in Central America in place of Mr. Borakas himself. He had told Carlos that the corporation needed a younger, more vigorous executive in Central America to carry forward the business plan. Carlos considered the offer but decided not to give up a six-figure job as a VP of a world-wide construction firm to face the animosity of Luis, his half-brother by blood.

Her father had a heart attack the following day. She remembered her confusion and sorrow when Corey and she took the next available plane to the Bay Area. Carlos joined them in taking her father's body to the Suarez Moncada family crypt in San Salvador. Her father was not yet sixty years old and he had worn himself out helping Leona dream her dream—and, oh, how, overjoyed he had been when near the first anniversary, Leona delivered a son, his first grandchild, whom they named Nicolas.

She then thought of Corey's tenderness in the difficult weeks that followed her father's death and then her joy in learning that she was pregnant again—this time with her daughter. Sure, she still ran her company. She moved its headquarters to Charlotte from Coral Gables to mother her children and she arranged with Margarita for her nurse maid to come up to take care of them while she was at work. She sometimes wondered if being at work was worth the time she lost with Corey and the children.

Without her father, it was a new work environment. Her travel was limited. She had to rely on agronomists in Central America to ride hard over the producers under contract and she delegated to them decision-making authority that only her father had exercised before. Leona called on Margarita for help in checking on the agronomist and Central American operations—but she lacked the special management insights and skills that her father had honed over his lifetime. And those assignments kept her away from San Salvador weeks at a time—weeks that Tio Umberto warned her were being used by Luis for his own purposes.

Part of her father's estate included some of the Suarez Moncada properties acquired after the agreement between grandfather and Mr. Borakas's father. The original fincas were deeded to Leona and held in trust for her, but the additional coffee, cotton, and sugar were in her father's name. Luis had maneuvered over the years to assume management of those additional properties and muddied up the waters of management rights after Mr. Borakas death. What Luis did not know was that father had carefully arranged with the Borakas bank that, once he passed, the title to the properties would revert to the bank, with the income destined for his grandchildren. Father had not had time to cue Leona in, but Margarita was—she had drawn up and filed the documents.

Leona remembered her father's uneasiness about his relationship with Luis, but could never identify anything specific. Luis was competent, efficient, and considerate. He accompanied his uncle on trips and to meetings, apparently content to be seen but not heard. On Mr. Borakas' death, he became the face of the Suarez Moncada business complex in San Salvador, representing and accompanying Leona to meetings and in handling business deals.

Leona dwelt on how difficult it had been for her after her father's death. She really wanted to be with her young family in Charlotte. True, she had the Salvadorian nanny to take care of her two infants, but she really wanted to be the nanny herself and share those precious moments with her husband. But she had a multinational business to run.

Since Kennedy's assassination, she had observed the gradual disappearance of interest in his great initiative, the Alliance for Progress and its support for the Central American Common Market. All the foreign policy attention had drifted to Vietnam. Most of her husband's former colleagues at the White House and in the State Department returned to academia or the private sector. And in Central America, the military leaders observing the change in priorities in Washington, consolidated their power and slowed progress in the Common Market except for projects in which they had special interest. Leona no longer hurried to Central America to participate in regional meetings.

Leona tried to spend as much time at home as possible. She delegated much of the day-to-day operations to her field agronomists and company managers, but there always seemed to be problems that her father had attended to that now required her personal attention—even after she called on Margarita's fine hand.

For almost three years, this was the way she ran a profitable multinational company. Then came the terrible 200-hour Soccer War between El Salvador and Honduras that suspended operations of the Common Market and disrupted production from many of the farms which supplied the lifeblood of her company. That disruption required her to spend weeks at a time away from her husband and children. She found herself spending more and more time at her father's house in San Benito, living across the hall from Margarita and her daughter Blanca.

She also found herself depending more on cousin Luis to help with Salvadoran producers whose operations were adversely affected by disruptions in the Common Market. Luis was always attentive and solved some difficult bottlenecks. He made it a practice to appear in public as much as possible at Leona's side or explaining one of her decisions or actions.

Tio Umberto and Margarita warned her several times that Luis had his own agenda and was building a cadre of discontents among the great families. They warned her that he was using her. She had dismissed their warning—until she was seated in the meeting yesterday watching him use her and employing Granmama's catechism to lull her into inaction.

CHAPTER 24

Now she knew she had to act. She turned on the bed-lamp and saw it was 2:00 A.M. less than twelve hours since Luis' meeting ended. She rose from bed, put on a silk dressing gown and walked into her adjoining sitting room-study. She was wide awake, no longer meandering through her life. She had recognized the trap she was in and how the ghosts of Granmama's catechism had put there.

She was furious with herself for sitting stoically through the proceedings and not taking issue with Luis. "How did I so underestimate him? Why did I disregard my father's, Margarita's and Tio Umberto's warnings?" she said painfully to the walls of her study. Then, with the acumen of a mature businesswoman, she pulled herself together and began planning what she would do to thwart Luis and redeem herself.

She made some notes, looked up some phone numbers and began with a phone call to her cousin Luis's home phone. After only one ring, his anxious wife picked up, half crying, "Is that you Luis?" "No dear. This is Leona. I 'm looking for Luis."

His anxious wife responded, "I have not seen him since breakfast yesterday. He has not called me, nor did he come home for dinner. I am very concerned. Do you know where he might be?"

Leona replied, "No, not at the minute. I was with him much of the afternoon and need to talk to him urgently. Call me if you hear anything."

Now, she knew that Luis had pushed the key button of his agenda and was working with his friends to spring his trap. Leona could hear him deliberately spelling out how "we" must act immediately to save "them" from themselves. It was Granmama's litany that had lulled her through the meeting.

Then she turned her chair around to face the short-wave radio on the side table. She dialed the call numbers of Tio Umberto-- Colonel Umberto Urdaneta, the longtime G-2 of the Army. He better than anyone else in the country would know what Luis was up to.

He had become her friend and counselor, always faithfully to her and her father. She knew at this critical moment, he was the only person in El Salvador to whom she could turn. In less than a minute, Tio Umberto answered.

Leona began, "Sorry *padrino* (godfather) for the early call." Padrino was the private name she called him.

He said, "I was about to call you *princesa* (princess)." Princesa was his private name for her.

"Oh?", she interjected.

"My agents advised me about the secret meeting of the Great Families that Luis called yesterday afternoon and I bugged the meeting room," he said to her.

"Then you know why I am so upset and need to talk to you. I have spent the several hours trying to figure out why I sat stoically by while Luis staged his meeting," she bemoaned.

"As I listened to the tapes I was waiting for you to challenge Luis—and I know many others in that room were too," he responded.

"The words seemed to lull me to sleep. I realize now that he was mouthing the same phrases on which Granmama had nursed me and that I had not realized were still coloring my approach to so many aspects of my life, especially dealing with the people I was trying to help. I finally exorcised her catechism from my thinking process and my soul and I need your advice on what I need to do to stop Luis," she said very deliberately.

"Princesa, you are too late to stop him. He is meeting downstair with the hard-line colonels, the men I warned you he was befriending. One of my adjutants is in the meeting and he sent me a message a short time ago that Luis has offered the unlimited support of the Great Families in preventing the election of anyone other than the colonel we nominated. He put money on the table and delivered to them a death list of people that the Great Families want eliminated," he advised her.

"But, Padrino, there was no discussion, much less a decision by anyone at that meeting anywhere close to authorizing Luis to make such an offer," she pleaded.

"Yes, I know. I listened to the tape twice. But, you give Luis an inch and he takes a mile. Princesa, your father and I warned you so many times not to trust him. He hates you and played you for a fool. Your father believed that your education in the United States and your years of working with him had prepared you to deal with him. I was not so sure," he continued.

"Luis has always known of your longing for affection from your Granmama, and learned all the phrases of her catechism of "us" and "them." When I heard his presentation at the meeting, I knew that he was in effect hypnotizing you into silence. He maliciously used your obsession with your grandmother to try to destroy you."

Leona sat upright and saw the full consequences of her acquiescence only a few hours ago.

"My adjutant tells me that my fellow colonels are tempted by the money and are discussing terms with Luis. He expects the meeting to continue through the night and that there will be a conclave of all us colonels in the mornings to formally reach an institutional accord. My guess is that Luis's offer will be accepted and that the corps will give a green light to our taking full control of the government and run the country as we did in the 1930's under General Martinez."

Leona gasped and said again, "The meeting never agreed to that."

"This is what your father and I feared Luis was planning and to use you in making it happen. I hope you realize how much your *primo hermano* resents you."

"We have no time to waste now. I am concerned for your safety right now. I advise you to leave the country before the meeting in the morning. I will send a car with the captain you know well to pick you, Margarita and her daughter Blanca up in about an hour. It is now 2:40 A.M. My car will be there in an hour to take you three to that small airstrip near Santa Tecla—the one used for spraying the crops. Your Piper cub is already there with approved flight plans to take you to San Jose, Guatemala. I have arranged for your car at the house in Antigua to be waiting for you at the airstrip in San Jose. No arguments," He signed off.

Leona almost shuttered as she put down the phone. She then hurried across the hall to Margarita's room. She knocked on the door and heard Margarita rousing herself. She called out to Margarita, "Wake up Blanca and pack a bag. We must be ready to leave the house in an hour."

"What did you just say?" queried Margarita as she opened the door.

Leona calmly repeated, "My dear, we are leaving the house in an hour. Colonel Urdaneta is sending a car to pick us up. Wake Blanca and pack a valise. I will pull some things in my overnight bag." Looking at her watch, she continued, "It is ten to three now. The car will be here at 4:00 A.M. I'll tell you all about the mess later."

CHAPTER 25

The car arrived on schedule. Leona, Margarita, and Blanca were waiting at the front door, accompanied by the butler whose wife had awakened him when she saw the lights on the second floor. Leona motioned for her companions to stand by until she was sure that the car was sent by Tio Humberto.

The guard at the door, another one of Tio Humberto's men, recognized the car and driver and opened the gate. Leona watched carefully and stayed inside the house until she saw Tio Humberto's captain move from the car to the front door.

He saluted Leona and said "Good morning, Senora. The Colonel advised me that all the necessary arrangements are in place and that we should move quickly."

Leona said, "Good morning captain. We are ready."

The butler carried three bags to the car as the captain escorted the ladies to the back seat. The butler came up to the car window where Leona was seated. Leona smiled as she said, "Thank you for getting up so early in the morning. We are going to the finca for a few days. You know how to reach me there. Take care of the house while we are away." Leona had spoken in a clear, loud voice so that anyone watching would hear her.

The captain jumped into the front seat and the car sped down the hill and then turned right on the highway to Santa Tecla. Forty minutes later they were at the small agricultural airstrip a few miles east of the town. The captain helped the ladies out of the car and as an afterthought said to Leona: "The Colonel said you would understand why he needed to stay at the barracks and asked me to make sure you ladies were safely on your way."

He led them to the four-seater Piper and said, "The pilot has the approved flight plan to San Jose, Guatemala. The car from Antigua will be waiting for you. The Colonel will be in touch with you as soon as circumstances permit. Have a pleasant flight."

Leona, Margarita and Blanca climbed aboard the Piper. Almost as an afterthought Leona smiled at the captain, "Thank you captain for your help. And please thank Colonel Underraga for making the arrangements. Tell him that I will be waiting for his call."

Margarita, Blanca and Leona strapped themselves in for the hour flight to San Jose. Margarita looked quizzically at Leona and received a discouraging look in return that said, "This is not the time to talk." Margarita returned a quizzical look but kept quiet. Blanca said, "Mommy I forgot my schoolbooks. I have homework for Monday," Margarita reassured her daughter, "I'll call the principal Monday morning and explain."

The pilot offered them a thermos of coffee and they were soon air bound.

Leona closed her eyes as the plane taxied down the short runway. In her mind's eye, she for a brief second saw her Granmama looking snuggly at her, but she pushed her aside and replaced it with her father's face, his soft brown eyes trying to console her. He led her back to the day in her dorm room he helped her get settled when she was starting her freshman year at Yale. She saw him so clearly and then heard him say, "Leona my dear, I am so glad that you chose Yale. It is a place that will make you think and let you grow."

Leona remembered replying, "You know father I really wanted to go to Neuchâtel to be close to Granmama. But I know and agreed that prep school better prepared me for Yale. I suspect the nuns at Neuchatel probably followed the same learning process as the nun in San Salvador rote Catholic learning, not forcing me to use my knowledge to think. Yes, I'm glad you insisted on prep school and that you agree with me about Yale."

Her father smiled as he continued, "Yale will be a special challenge for you. Leona you are a wealthy young woman who will inherit my banking resources as well as the Suarez Moncada properties. It is not a great fortune, but you will be among the wealthiest in our country. You can use your money for good or for mercenary purposes. You can help your country and its people, or you can serve yourself. I urge you to use your years at Yale to clarify what you want to do with your money and your life. Only you can do that."

Leona interrupted, "Ever since Miss Jones took me to the finca for the first time

I have wanted to help the finca families and all those Salvadorans who need help. I want to do positive things to improve my country."

Her father said thoughtfully, "That pleases me and you have a good start. Your years here should teach you how to find responsible ways to achieve those goals. You are not only going to learn from books and professors but also from the variety of students you meet from different backgrounds and social groups. This is also a great place to learn about the world and your role in it. Give yourself time to think and also enjoy life, but don't think only of yourself but of others with whom you will be sharing this tremendous opportunity."

She could almost hear him advising her, "Our world is changing in ways that we can barely appreciate today. Technology and science are transforming everything and modern communications carry the news of those changes to every corner of the country. The common people in poor countries like ours will want the benefits of the changes in countries like United States and they will not for long accept the status quo. Your education provides you a unique opportunity to learn how to work with people to channel change constructively— to build a new future in which they and we can participate together in improving living standards and sharing the governance of our country not turning back the clock in a futile attempt to prevent the inevitable change from taking place."

"Think my dear what your education is all about. Let it focus not merely on you and enhancing yourself, but on conserving and advancing the world. The true conservative must understand the changes that communications and technology inevitably causing to the essence of our life and that think of everything you can possibly do to harness those changes to improve the world in which we all must coexist."

She remembered almost verbatim his saying, "My hope is that you will be thinking about the ways and means for improving the world in which you will be living. Never forget that it is a world not merely of you and us but of you and them. Consider how best you and they can best live comfortably together. Listen to them, not merely talk to them."

Then he added, 'For the first time in your life, you will be living in an urban setting. New Haven is a city with problems of poverty. Take the time to observe how people interact with each other and how they try to help those in need—and try to learn what works and what is only a waste of time and money. Don't be afraid to face reality and keeping asking yourself as you try to help people: did you do it for them or for yourself? Put yourself in their place and ask yourself: if I were in need, would I trust those trying to help me? Remember our experiences at the finca."

"My dear, how you deal with people is as important as what you do to help them. Never stop asking yourself what you can do to enhance your interests in the context of change and what you should have to do to reach out to them, give them a voice and encourage them to join with in building institutions that broaden their - and your stake in a world in which both of us have to live together."

That day at Yale she heard her father in the context of Granmama's "we" and "they." That morning on the Piper Cub, she heard her father on a totally wavelength— almost the antithesis to Granmama. His counsel was the essence of what she should have said to counter Luis at the meeting. Many of those in the room would have understood and joined her.

With every thought, she was seeing more clearly how she had unthinkingly let words and phrases that she had heard so often from Granmama lull her into silence. The woman whose affection and admiration she so ardently strove to receive, led her to betray her own aspirations.

The face in the mirror was right.

CHAPTER 26

It was still dark when the plane landed. All the necessary arrangements in Guatemala had been made so that when they left the plane, the car to take them to Antigua was waiting. There were no customs or immigration formalities at the small agricultural landing strip. So the three ladies just walked to the car where the long-time family chauffeur held open the door. They settled into the backseat while the chauffeur placed their small valises in the trunk. It took less than two hours to reach Leona's home in the colonial jewel city.

The home located near the Alcaldia (City Hall) had been in her Granmama's families for centuries and was given to Granmama on her marriage. Leona's father had purchased it from Granmama in the late 1950's when the old lady decided that she wanted to spend the rest of her life in

Neuchatel and needed additional cash to finance her lifestyle there.

When her father purchased this piece of Granmama, he restored it to its past glory. He strengthened the foundations, put on new roofs, rebricked the interior patios, replaced the panoply of semi-tropical plants and brought in new trees for the orchard behind the two-story main house. He built a new two-car garage, with mechanically controlled doors, installed the latest electrical and plumbing equipment and put in a small power plant for the times public services were out. He refurbished it for easy living. He did it for Leona and she loved the house—its layout and interior patios reminded her of the mansion in which she grew up.

It was not yet 8:00 AM, when the sedan approached the garage doors carved out of the thick adobe walls. The doors like magic flew open and the car disappeared inside. The three ladies were met by the aged housekeeper Lupe, at the corridor leading from the garage to the main living quarters.

"I just learned a few hours ago that you were coming. The beds in your bedrooms have been made up and we have breakfast ready for you, but I will need most of the day to get the rest of the house ready for you. When you let me know how long you plan to stay, I will need to go to the market for more food and supplies."

"Don't worry Lupe. We plan to rest for the day and will want a simple dinner tonight. I don't expect to stay for more than tonight and tomorrow. Please don't worry about getting food and supplies—we will make do. I'm sorry that we gave so little notice, but I made a last-minute decision. And I don't want people to know that Margarita, Blanca and I are here. We want to rest. Please tell the staff to say nothing of this visit."

"Oh, yes, senora, I will instruct the staff to say nothing. You rest. I will have dinner ready for you whenever you are ready. We will be very quiet so you can rest. You can count on us."

Lupe led the way to the living room. She motioned to a maid to take the valises across the patio to the stairway up to the second floor where the master suite and Margarita's and Blanca's room were situated. Leona nodded her thanks, and Lupe retired.

Leona then put her arm on Margarita's shoulder and smiled, "I have much to talk about with you. Yesterday was traumatic for me and I made a horrendous mistake. Last night I tried to understand what happened. I'm still grappling with myself. I want to share my thoughts with you, but I need to make some arrangements and then get some rest before we talk. I will need your help in the difficult days that lie ahead. So let's have some breakfast and turn in for the day. We'll talk when we get up."

They walked into the adjoining dining room for breakfast.

When they finished, Margarita and Blanca went to their bedrooms while Leona went into the office, where her short-wave set was situated. Her first call was to Neil Adams in Miami. He was the CEO of the charter plane company she used for most of her overseas business flights.

She dialed his call number and received an immediate answer.

"Morning, this is Leona Borakas. Is Neil available?"

The voice said, "Yes, he is right here," and put Neil on the line.

"Leona, I'm surprised to hear from so

early on a Saturday morning. What can I do for you?"

"Morning Neil. I need your help. I am in Antigua and need to get back to Charlotte tomorrow. Do you have a charter available for me and two other ladies tomorrow. I need urgently to get back home."

"You mean Antigua, Guatemala?" he asked.

"Yes, Guatemala," she replied.

"Just a second. Let me look at the locations and schedules of my planes." There was a pause of a several minutes before he continued, "I have a plane coming back from Managua early Sunday morning. I can route it through Aurora. It should be there about 11:00 AM and ready for departure before noon. Would that work for you?"

"Couldn't be better. Should we pick it

up at the private plane area of Aurora?" queried Leona.

"Yes indeed. Who will be flying with you so I can prepare the manifest and make arrangements with the officials at Aurora?"

"It is a party of three. Margarita, her daughter and me. You have all the passport, visa and other details of both Margarita and me—and Blanca Margarita's daughter is on Margarita's Salvadoran passport."

"Just a minute. Let me check my records." Another pause before Neil answered, "A okay. I see all the information we need for Guatemalan and US immigration. I will take care of the flight plan and other details. The plane will be waiting for you before noon tomorrow. We'll have you home for dinner Sunday night."

"Thank you, Neil. There will be an extra bonus for your help," as Leona signed off.

Next, she called home to her Corey. He answered almost immediately, "Hello, dear I've been waiting for your call. Are you all right?" he responded.

Leona sighed, "It's big mess down here. It's a long story. I sat by and … I am sorry for what is happening. I'll tell you all after I get home. Are the children well? Has anything happened since we talked Thursday evening?"

"When do you expect to be coming home?"

"Tomorrow evening. I have arranged with Neil for one of his charters to pick us up at noon tomorrow—and Neil says that we'll be home for dinner,"

"Who are we?' Corey queried.

"Margarita and Blanca are with me. We are fleeing from what I let happen."

"So it's a political mess you got yourself into, and I can guess who helped you get out of El Salvador."

"Yes, dear, I walked into a trap that Luis set for me and I just sat by. Tio Umberto got us out."

Corey was reassuring, "I am glad you are safe. I'm eager to hear what happened. It may be the basis for another of my class lectures."

"Just one more thing, Margarita and Blanca will be staying with us. Please have the guest rooms ready for them. Love you dear. Give the children a hug for me. See you tomorrow night."

Her third call was to her uncle in Panama. She dialed his number and waited minutes until a custodian picked up. In Spanish she asked for her uncle. "No senora, he is not here today, but I will get the officer on duty today to speak with you."

After a short wait, the officer of the day came on, "Yes, how may I help you?"

"Thank you, senor, this is Leona Borakas, his niece, I need to talk to him urgently. Can you connect me to him?"

"Yes, senora Borakas, he left me a number in case of emergency. And I can patch him in. Just a minute please."

After a short wait, her uncle's voice said, "Leona?"

"Yes, Tio, it is I. I am so sorry to bother you, but things in El Salvador are coming apart. I had to come to Antigua for personal safety."

"But you are all right?'

"Physically fine. I'll explain what happened on Monday. But I need some immediate action to protect our assets in El Salvador. I need you to immediately freeze all our accounts and put a stop order on any withdrawals by my cousin Luis Suarez Moncada effective right now."

"Yes, I will advise the officer of the day to take action as soon as this call is over," was her uncle's reply.

"And", continued Leona, "Advise our lawyers in San Salvador that Luis has no authority to act for the Bank or the Suarez Moncada Borakas properties. Administration of those funds and properties have been transferred to corporate headquarters in Charlotte until further notice."

"Yes, Leona, I get a sense of what is happening. I will see that everything is taken care of this morning. I am looking forward to hearing from you Monday. I take it that you have left San Salvador en route to Charlotte?"

"Yes uncle, I am in Antigua and

should be home tomorrow evening if all goes as planned."

"Take care. Our love to you, Corey and the children. Bye."

As she ended her call to uncle and was about to go to bed, she received an incoming call from San Salvador—from Tio Umberto. As she tuned in, the voice at the other end said, "Princesa, is that you?"

"Yes Padrino, we are in Antigua."

"I don't have much time, but I want you to arrange with the charter flight company you use to get you back to Charlotte tomorrow. I am off for the meeting with my colleagues."

She almost cried, "Padrino, thank you. You must have been up all night. I can't thank you enough for taking care of Margarita, Blanca and me in the midst of your dealing with the situation there that I helped create. I wanted you to know that we arrived without incident and that I have already arranged for the charter flight tomorrow at noon."

She continued, "I have been doing a lot of soul searching to find answers for my acquiescence yesterday. I have a lot to be sorry for. That's for one of our private talks. I just want to repeat that I am ashamed of my silence. You listened to the discussion yesterday and heard me sitting by as Luis used Granmama's words to lull me into indifference. You know that the meeting did not agree to any extreme measures, only undefined support for the military. I would not have agreed to investing anyone with dictatorial powers or funding death squads. I now see the damage that my inaction has caused. I still hope it is not too late."

Tio Umberto's only reply was, "I hope so, too."

CHAPTER 27

Leona then went up to her bedroom for an uneasy sleep for the rest of the day. In her reverie she began speculating about the events in San Salvador and their effect on her returning to El Salvador and her company's operations there. She began assessing how complicated the situation had become for not only herself but also Margarita and Blanca.

She said to herself over and over through those uneasy hours, "You have no one to blame but yourself. You thought yourself so savvy, so well-prepared that you could handle Luis and just about any problem yourself and you never bothered to consult anyone before the meeting, not even Tio Umberto or Margarita."

She also realized with all her education how dependent she had really been on the guidance of her father. He, not Granmama, had been the rock on which she had built her life. As she rose from bed to shower and dress, she finally admitted to herself, "If my father had been alive, yesterday afternoon would probably not have happened. He would have worked with Tio Umberto to prevent the meeting from ever taking place. My God, I have been so blind." The truth hurt.

Late in the afternoon she crossed the hall and knocked on Margarita's door. "Are you awake?" When she received no answer, she walked downstairs and across the patio to the living room where Margarita was reading and Blanca was playing with one of the dogs.

Leona interrupted, "Afternoon, so good to see you."

Margarita looking up and said, "Did you get some rest? Are you feeling better?"

"Yes. I never fell into a restful sleep. Too many things running around in my head."

The housekeeper Lupe appeared. "Good afternoon, ladies. Sorry to interrupt, but we have prepared the early dinner for Blanca and it is ready in the dining room."

Margarita smiled, "Thank you Lupe. Blanca is very tired from the trip and I want to get her to bed early tonight."

Blanca seemed delighted at the news and followed Lupe without a word.

"Well, are you ready to tell me what this is all about?" Margarita asked.

"I don't really know where to start. There is so much to talk out," Leona replied as she settled into a chair facing Margarita. "You remember how uneasy I was when I left for the meeting. I became even more concerned when I saw Luis seated at the head of the table. I was the only woman present. I looked around the table and there were 20 of us from the Great

Families, most of them second or third sons—only a few of whom I had interacted with before. I had hardly settled in my seat when Luis welcomed us."

"His first words were that our families and our national traditions were under attack by the radical 'them.' They are agitating to disrupt operations at many of the fincas and plantations and causing political unrest. We are facing elections this weekend that threaten to undermine the political status quo that has enabled our allies in the military to protect our interests."

"He then ran through the old drill that we are the families who brought Christ and civilization to the country and that we have a sacred responsibility to ensure that the people we civilized and redeemed do not jeopardize what we have given them by making the wrong political choices."

Margarita looked Leona squarely in

the eye "Leona, you didn't let him continue?" And, then she read Leona's eyes and said, "Oh, my dear, you did. You heard him repeating all those words Granmama heaped on you in the library and the classroom. Let me guess. Luis said, 'We have the responsibility to protect the people who depend on us for guidance and their livelihood.'

"Yes," Leona cut in. "I just sat there listening like a child, not to Luis, but to Granmama. He ran on and on about our duty as the born leaders of the country to act before the radical 'them' subverted the progress of the last two decade and public order. My mind told me that Luis was hogwash but something else inside hypnotized me into silence."

"Then a few of his cronies supported him urging us to advise our military allies that they had our full support to take such action that may be appropriate to prevent the situation from getting out of hand. I saw several of the others looking to me for some sort of reaction, before I could react, Luis said that the meeting agreed on the urgent need to reassure our military allies and abruptly adjourned."

Margarita just stared ahead as Leona continued, "So, I gather Luis went to his radical friends in the military who have been working to restore a dictatorship and offered them the support of the Families—support far beyond the words used at the meeting. Money and death squads eliminate people like you and me who have thwarted Luis's grasping the Suarez Moncada wealth. So, Tio Umberto got us out of San Salvador before the colonels reached a decision on Luis's offer of support."

"Margarita you are so right," Leona confirmed "I stopped hearing the discussion, I was driven into myself. I acquiesced to Luis's proposal, visualizing some form of mediation. Late last night I had to confess to myself that I should have stood up to him in the meeting. I realized that Luis and his cronies really intended to unleash the Army to liquidate 'them' as their grandfather had supported General Martinez in 1931. My educated self, thought that we were past that, but I underestimated Luis. My mistake let the clock be turned back, mañana became yesterday."

"When I tried to sleep, I relived those years in the mansion and my obsession with Granmama. She was my idol—the only senior woman in my life. Well, I have come to grips with my obsession and am exorcising her catechism from my life. I only hope it is not too late."

"I told you last night when I came home that I was not pleased with the meeting, my silence at it or the results.

When I looked in the mirror of my dressing table the face looking back at me was my own when I entered Yale—and that face told me that afternoon I had betrayed everything I wanted to stand for."

"All last night I relived our years at the mansion, Granmama and her catechism of "we" and "they"—the same words I listened to Luis mouthing at the meeting. I also faced my feelings for my father and finally acknowledged him for the good wise man that he was, how he, not the Suarez Moncadas, truly loved me and served as my emotional and intellectual guide."

"This clearing of mind leaves lots of things to be reworked between us. You are most dear to me, much more than my oldest and truest friend. We both know this friendship is reinforced by our blood relationship. Perhaps because of the shadow of Granmama I have never acknowledged that you are my aunt, the incredibly wonderful gift of a terrible rape by my savage uncle Arturo of a defenseless child - as much a Suarez Moncada as I am. I've known that since our first visit to the finca when one of the finca girls there told me that my uncle Arturo was your father. Since I had not been told by Granmama, I never said anything. I didn't have the character of my father and Uncle Felipe to embrace and support you as a family member. Well, now, I ask your forgiveness. Blanca and you are part and parcel of my life and my family."

Margarita teared up as she said, "I never expected to hear that from you Leona because of Granmama. Even after grandfather recognized me as a member of his family, Granmama rejected me. She never would accept that her eldest and favorite son Arturo would be accused of raping a twelve-year old lowly finca girl. In Granmama' logic: Arturo may have given the girl a sexual favor because she begged for it, but dear Arturo imposing himself on a child, never! She would never forgive me for being—and she detested grandfather's decision to have my mother live in her house—even as a kitchen maid. And she blamed my mother's brothers for Arturo's death. I thought that your devotion to Granmama would always be a wall between us. Thank God it is gone."

Leona said, "We have a lot of time ahead of us. And I plan to have my aunt around to cherish for the rest of my life."

Leona walked toward Margarita gave her a deep hug and a kiss—and Margarita hugged and kissed back.

"There are couple of more things I should tell you. I talked to Tio Umberto this morning and he decided to get us out of Guatemala tomorrow. I called my charter company and arranged for a plane to pick us up at noon tomorrow. I also talked to Corey, and he is preparing the guest rooms for Blanca and you."

"I also told Tio Umberto what I now understand what happened at the meeting yesterday. He cut me off and said that he knew exactly what transpired—his team had bugged the room. He then told me that Luis advised his cronies that he had a free hand to support the military in doing everything necessary to avoid a political defeat tomorrow and ensure the maintenance of the status quo. Luis has been meeting all night with his colonel friends. Tio Umberto said Luis included you and me on the hit list he left with the colonels for the death squads. He also informed me that a conclave of the key colonels has been called for this afternoon to decide the Army's response to whatever Luis has proposed. He said he would call me when a decision is reached."

Then, Leona said, "We need to have our dinner soon. We should turn in early since we will be leaving tomorrow morning by 9:00 A.M. to catch the charter at noon. I talked to Corey, and he is having the guest rooms readied for Blanca and you."

Leona called to Lupe. When Lupe appeared, Leona asked. "Can you have dinner ready in a half hour?"

"Of course," was the reply.

"And please ask the driver to be ready to take us to Aurora at 9:00 A.M. tomorrow morning. We'll have breakfast at 8:00 A.M. We are flying home so no need for any further meals. We will let you get back to your usual routine."

Lupe said, "I am sorry that you are leaving so soon, but I will take care of everything. Would you like a cocktail before dinner?"

Leona looked at Margarita, who smiled. "Yes, thank you, Lupe. Bring us a bottle of scotch, soda, and some ice."

Once Leona mixed the drinks, the two ladies sat down next to each other on the sofa. Leona said, "Just one more thing. I called my uncle in Panama, froze all the Salvador accounts and asked him to advise our lawyers to inform all our clients and suppliers that effective Monday all Salvadoran business will operate out of headquarters—Luis is unemployed!"

"Here's to us," said Margarita.

"Yes, Aunt Margarita, here's to us!"

CHAPTER 28

After dinner, Leona said, "Come with me to the office. I need to talk to Tio Humberto and find out what was decided today."

Leona dialed Tio Umberto's call letters on the short-wave set. She tried several times before she got a response. "Is the Colonel there?"

"No. He is still in the meeting. This is Captain Sepulveda. He told me to tell you that he would be calling you as soon as the meeting ends."

"Thank you, Captain. Let me tell you how much I appreciated your help earlier this morning. Everything went as planned. We are so grateful. We will wait for his call."

Margarita and Leona then settled

back in their chairs. Margarita noted, "That is one long meeting. The discussions must be hot and heavy."

The ladies began reading but fell asleep in their chairs. They were awakened near midnight by the screeching of the short-wave.

Leona half-asleep responded, "Princesa here. Is that you Padrino?"

"Yes, Princesa. This is Padrino a very tired Padrino. It was a difficult heated discussion. Luis and his cronies offered my brethren and me millions of colones to disrupt the elections tomorrow if the results do not ensure victories by our candidates. He said that the money would be available no matter what actions we colonels decided to take. Luis used your silence to claim that you were in favor of the military taking necessary action. He also said that he was authorized to provide additional colones if the opponents of the status quo were eliminated, and he passed around a list of names. I can confirm that Margarita and your names are on the list. Luis also bragged to us that he will soon be taking personal control of all Suarez Moncada properties and be able to show his additional appreciation to his friends in the future."

Leona gasped and Margarita took a deep breath.

"After Luis left, we colonels had a lengthy, sometimes heated, institutional discussion. Many colonels supported me, but the lure of the money that Luis placed on the table weighed heavy in my colleagues' minds. A bird in the hand outweighed my argument that the Army's optimal position was to let the elections take place, stay in the barracks, and use our institutional power to influence the policies of whatever government was elected. I emphasized that, without turning to us, any government would have very limited resources—especially trained administrators—to keep the public sector afloat, much less introduce many changes. I warned them that, if the opposition didn't believe that the electoral process offered any hope for change, it would choose armed insurrection and lay waste to our country. I told my colleagues that we had to avoid any action that might lead to civil warfare. In the end, the colonels elected to take that risk and accept Luis's proposal. I regretted the decision, but as a member of the institution, I will adhere to it."

Leona cut in, "Thank you Padrino for the grim news."

Tio Umberto cut right back in, "Before we finish this night, I want to tell you how much I valued my long friendship with your father. We worked together for nearly thirty years. He showed me how technology and communications was changing our traditional socio-economic structures. He convinced me that for orderly change we with power had to embrace the change process, open up economic opportunity, educate people and given them a stake to ever broadening segments of our people, educate them, give them a stake in the change process and enable them to improve their living conditions. He showed me how complex the process will be, but convinced me that it would be a long, difficult path. I regret that you Princesa did not act like your father. You let Luis, with his message of yesterday, take the initiative from you. If you had come to my institution with your father's vision and pledged your resources to help my institution join in the undertaking, I think I could have brought them along. For you had the financial resources to allay our fears of change."

"Well, it is too late now. Regretfully for our country—for us personally and all we aspired to do. Your inaction and the decision of my institution have made our tomorrow a repetition of the past. Yes, manana is yesterday."

"Have a safe trip tomorrow. It may be a long time before we embrace each other again."

Made in the USA
Middletown, DE
21 July 2023

35545913R00220